Broken

Damaged Hearts book 1

Margaux Paris

Broken

Broken

Copyright © 2025 by Margaux Paris.

Hardcover ISBN: 978-1-7643194-3-0

This book is a work of fiction. Names, characters, businesses, organisations, Places, events and incidents either are the product of the author's imagination or are used fictitiously. Any resemblance to actual persons, living or dead, events, or locales is entirely coincidental.

Please note: British English spelling has been used throughout this book.

Book design by Margaux Paris
Cover design by Margaux Paris
Edited by CJ Editing

First Edition: January 2025

Broken

Broken

DEDICATION

For the ones who highlight the filth,
fall for the red flags like they're rose petals,
and mutter *"he's perfect"*.

There were monsters in the room—
but he had better manners.

Broken

Broken

Trigger Warning

Broken contains mature themes and content that may be distressing to some readers.
This includes references to sexual assault, physical assault, physical abuse, emotional manipulation, psychological trauma, obsessive behaviour, and mental health struggles.
The story is intended for adult readers and explores complex, often confronting emotional dynamics.
Please read with care.

Broken

Broken

Authors Note

Broken is the first book in the *Damaged Hearts Duet*.

This story is only half the journey. The emotional conclusion continues in *Flawed*, and is not intended to be skipped.

This is a duet about love, obsession, trauma, and the mess we make in trying to survive them.

It was never meant to be simple.

Broken

Playlist

Ashley- **Escape the Fate**

Pittsburgh **- The Amity Affliction**

Don't Lean On Me **- The Amity Affliction**

Criminals - **DMA's**

Tears Don't Fall – **Bullet for My Valentine**

Alright – **Hollywood Undead**

Last Resort (Reimagined)– **Falling in Reverse**

Monster – **Gabbie Hanna**

All I Want – **Kodaline**

The Bitch Song – **Bowling for Soup**

Love Like War – **All Time Low (Vic Fuentes)**

Just Pretend – **Bad Omen**

Broken

Broken

CHAPTER 1

Sweat beads on my forehead, a result of the adrenaline coursing through me, intensified by his proximity. One of his hands grips mine against the wall, while the other wraps around my throat— tight enough to silence me, but still allowing me to breathe. In through my nose, out through my mouth. I remind myself to steady my breathing before I lose consciousness. His lips brush gently against my shoulder, then follow the curve with

Broken

his nose. He bends slightly, and the hand not constricting my throat finds its way to my inner thigh, his fingertips teasing as they glide up my skin and lift my skirt. With the hem adjusted to stay in place, he cups me, sending shivers down my legs as his lips find my ear.

"Tell me you want it," he murmurs, his tongue dancing along the shell. I'm too overwhelmed to respond—unable to speak or breathe—completely entranced by his presence. His fingers trace the outline of my underwear before slipping inside, circling my clit with slow precision. His breath is hot and heavy in my ear as he rasps, "You feel as good as I knew you would."

When he pushes a finger deeper, my body tenses. I realise I'm not getting enough air, leaving me dizzy and faint. He tightens his grip on my neck for a moment, a reminder of his control, then slides his finger deeper. I clench around him and he chuckles.

"You're so fucking tight," he growls against my skin.

As he releases my throat, I gasp for air, a cry

escaping my lips. In a flash, he tears my panties apart, the delicate lace no match for his strength, and shoves the remnants into my mouth.

His hands wrap around my wrists, pulling them above my head and pinning them against the wall. With one hand holding me captive, he unbuttons his jeans with the other, pushing them down to his knees. His cock springs free, pressing against my thigh—hard and demanding.

I feel him shift his weight as he leans back slightly. My eyes are drawn to the way he spits into his hand, then strokes himself rhythmically. Once satisfied, he leans back into me, hand sliding along my hips as he lifts one of my legs to wrap around his waist. I feel the tip of his arousal brush against me.

Then, in a calm voice that chills me, he whispers in my ear, "Are you ready, banana?"

But I'm frozen. My mind screams for my body to resist becoming his puppet as he starts to push forward —

I jolt awake, my heart hammering against my ribs like a trapped bird. A thin sheen of sweat clings to my

Broken

skin, and the sheets are twisted and damp around me. For a moment, I'm disoriented, unsure of where I am or even who I am.

The room slowly comes into focus—the familiar glow of the streetlight filtering through the blinds, the teetering stack of books on my nightstand, the faint scent of lavender from the diffuser. But the dread clings to me, heavy and suffocating.

In frustration, I rip off my sweat-soaked shirt and throw it against the wall. I know this nightmare too well, though it hasn't haunted me in months. Usually, stress triggers them, but I can't pinpoint anything right now that would explain this.

I moved three months ago, trying to take back control of my life. I won't let this be a setback. I'm stronger than whatever my subconscious tries to throw at me.

I rise from bed, searching for confidence I don't feel, and turn on the shower. I hope the water will wash away not just the sweat but the memories and lingering fear. While waiting for it to warm up, I make the regrettable decision to look in the mirror.

Broken

The reflection is stark: skin paler than usual, frantic hazel eyes haunted by a different life, and a tangle of mahogany hair falling past my shoulders. I'm a fucking mess.

The rest of my day goes by without drama. Wearing my favourite Nikes with glittery silver swooshes, I follow my usual routine: grabbing coffee from the café just half a block away, then taking the scenic route home to burn off some of the leftover adrenaline.

But when I get back, my front door suddenly feels like a fortress.

I stand in the hallway, keys in hand, staring at my own door like it's the gateway to hell. Last night's nightmare is messing with my head, and now the idea of stepping inside fills me with unease. This is supposed to be my safe space, but all I can picture is that shadowy figure from my dream, waiting for me.

Get a fucking grip. It was just a dream.

Inside, everything looks just how I left it, which—oddly—unsettles me. Still, I check every room. White walls, pale timber tiles underfoot, soft coffee-coloured carpet in the bedrooms. Solid. Safe.

Broken

I kick off my shoes and grab my laptop from the kitchen counter.

I fire off an email to my former therapist, wondering if she might have insight into why I'm having nightmares again without a clear trigger. I say "former" because I'm not actively in therapy anymore, though Jeanie helped me through my agoraphobia for over three years. Her support, especially during my move to Sydney, was life-changing.

Now, I send her weekly emails—post-adjustment therapy, we call it.

I curl up on the corner of my L-shaped couch and spend the next hour scrolling freelance job sites. I never thought I'd end up editing fan-fiction, but here I am. It started when I stumbled across a self-publishing site. Some of the stories were great, but the formatting made my editor-brain twitch. So I offered help—for a small fee.

Soon, I found platforms that connect freelance editors with authors. I don't do it for the money—hell, I underbid most of the competition—but I love reading. There's something grounding about stepping

Broken

into someone else's imagination.

If I don't find anything new, I dig back into my current project:

What if a billionaire dominant got bitten by a vampire?

Not exactly Pulitzer stuff, but I've learned more about blood kinks than I ever thought possible—and now I need to know how it ends.

The intercom buzzes, making me jump and lose my place.

Who the hell could that be?

It's 6:30 on a Saturday night.

"Hello?"

"There's a Ms. Williams here to see you," the concierge says. "Who?"

"She says she's your brother's girlfriend."

I laugh. Tyler, my brother, is a certified fuckboy. If she thinks she's his girlfriend, she's delusional. Still, I can't resist a good bimbo moment so I tell the concierge to send her up.

The door opens to a bottle-blonde in a micro skirt and a top that barely qualifies as clothing. Yep—she

Broken

knows Tyler.

"I'm Ash. You must be Ty's baby sister," she chirps.

I roll my eyes. At twenty, I'm hardly a baby—just eighteen months younger than Ty—but he loves calling me that. Classic overprotective brother.

She hands me a bag, and I realise I haven't even introduced myself.

"I'm Ally. And I gotta say—I'm surprised, but not shocked that you brought gifts."

"He figured you wouldn't sign for delivery. Since I was coming to Sydney, I offered to bring it. I was told to leave it downstairs, but I wanted to meet you."

I smile despite myself. I usually hate when Ty spends money on me, but already knowing whats inside the box fills me with excitement.

Opening it slowly to savour the moment, I find the most perfect pair of purple glitter high-top Chucks.

God, I love that man.

I've been obsessed with glitter sneakers since my first pair of light-up Skechers at nine. Everyone thought it was just a phase—but eleven years later, I'm still swooning over every sparkly step.

Broken

"Well... they're interesting," Ash comments, unimpressed.

"They're perfect," I say dreamily.

"Come in—and thanks for bringing them. Can I get you a drink?"

"No. I'm actually here to take you out."

Wait, what?

There's no way my overbearing brother agreed to this. Is she trying to bond with me? *Gross.*

"That's sweet, but I have some work..."

"Don't be a pussy. Put on your hooker heels and let's go."

Okay, rude. She seemed cool at first, but maybe she's jealous Tyler spoils me.

I'm about to shut her down—but then I pause.

Why not?

I moved here to reinvent myself. Normal people go out. Socialise.

New city. New me.

And honestly? I'd pay to see Ty's face when she tells him she took me out.

"Give me ten minutes to get ready."

Broken

"Just don't wear those hideous shoes," she mutters.

Noted. Ash has no filter. This should be interesting.

CHAPTER 2

Two hours later, I'm at a bar with Ash, her cousin, and her friends. Apparently, hen's night is just an excuse for women to dress like hookers. I feel totally out of place in my skinny jeans and a black tank top with tie-up straps. I left my purple Chucks at home but—much to Ash's horror—I'm wearing gold glitter sneakers.

Broken

They're all closer to shitfaced than tipsy and have started in on me again for not drinking. I've never really gotten along with alcohol in public, and I'm okay with that. Ash, getting more sarcastic with every sip, claims I must be adopted because I'm not as fun as my brother—who she drunkenly admits she's in love with. This is definitely not going to end well for her.

I decide I need a break from these women and excuse myself, heading over to the bar to grab some water from the self-serve station at the end. I really need a good reason to escape this disaster.

As I'm brainstorming excuses, I notice a large figure approaching from the side, stepping a little too far into my personal space. He's probably around 6'2" and reeks of whiskey—like, a lot of whiskey. Then he says something that completely throws me off:

"You look like you suck good cock."

What the fuck?

My opinion of men might not be great, but surely they can't all be this awful. I must have misheard him.

"Pardon me?" I manage, sounding more confident than I actually feel.

Broken

Assertive men really freak me out, and this one in particular is making me feel super uneasy. Deep down, I know my mind might be overreacting, but I can't shake the feeling that I should trust my gut on this one.

"Your lips are so pouty; they'd look great around my cock." His gaze lingers on my lips, and bile rises in my throat.

I freeze, panic creeping in—but then, laughter erupts beside me. A deep, genuine sound that fills the air and eases some of my tension. There's something about the guy in front me that keeps my gaze locked on him. I'm still on edge, worried that if I look away for even a second, the creep might lunge.

"Is that really how you speak to women?" the laughter continues, wrapping around me like a warm blanket.

"Not only is that disrespectful as fuck, but you're freaking her out." The voice beside me is smooth and calm, with a watered-down accent.

The creep doesn't even have the decency to look embarrassed. He moves closer, forcing me to back up until I hit the bar. But the man beside me stands up instantly, placing a firm hand on the guy's chest and pushing him back to a more respectful distance. I'm still in a daze, panic holding me tight, unable to fully process what's happening.

"Seriously, dude. Leave."

The creep glances between us before deciding I'm not worth the trouble. He turns and stalks off.

A breath slips from my lungs before I even noticed it was there. As I watch him walk away, someone steps into my line of sight. Warm fingers brush against my upper arm, making me flinch and snap out of my trance. He quickly pulls his hand back, and I look up.

Dark brown hair, shorter on the sides and spiked on top. A strong jawline with a five o'clock shadow. Sinfully full lips. Beautifully tanned skin. A tattoo peeking out from under his collar. The lighting is too dim to catch the colour of his eyes, but they radiate warmth. His expression shifts from casual to concerned.

"Are you okay?" he asks, almost like he's repeating himself.

"Yeah, I'm fine. Thanks for… um, intervening."

Broken

But am I really okay? I've been around Tyler and his friends enough to handle brazen guys, but that creep really rattled me.

"You look a bit pale. Want to step outside for some fresh air?"

"Um, no, I'm good. I'm just about to say goodbye to my friends and catch an Uber home."

"You sure?"

He's tall—around 6'3", maybe 6'4"—but he keeps a respectful distance. I can't help noticing his broad shoulders and the way his simple black T-shirt clings to his chest and biceps, with dark tattoos snaking down his left arm.

Fuck, this guy is hot.

Where the fuck did that thought come from? I haven't been interested in guys in years, but something about this one has me curious. He's looking at me again with that expectant gaze. Shit—he asked me something.

"Yes, thank you. And thanks again for scaring off the creep."

"Anytime. I'm Jax, by the way."

Broken

"Nice to meet you, Jax."

That makes him chuckle a bit; he knows I'm dodging giving my name, and he finds it amusing. With that jawline and those lips, he's probably used to women swooning. I need to make my escape before I embarrass myself even more—but I can't seem to make my legs move.

Suddenly, I'm shoved from behind, and Jax grabs my arm to steady me. My hands land on his chest. It's firm and warm, and I can't help wanting to explore. His scent is intoxicating—sandalwood mixed with something citrusy. I take a deep breath to inhale more.

Oh my god. Did I just sniff him?

Ash's whiny voice snaps me out of my inappropriate thoughts.

"Where have you been?"

"Sorry, I got distracted," I reply as she glances up at the man behind me.

"Nice job, Ally. He's hot."

Christ on a bike! This girl needs a fucking filter—or at least a muzzle. My cheeks flush, and irritation bubbles up. Jax just laughs behind me.

Broken

"So, Ally. That's a pretty name."

"I apologise; I shouldn't have assumed you two know each other. She's been a loser all night anyway." Ash adds/

That's it. Fake tits is officially on my shit-list. I flash her my fakest smile before making introductions.

"Jax, this is Ash. She's a friend of my brother's."

Ash quickly corrects me. "Actually, I'm her brother's *girlfriend.*"

"That's still up for debate. My brother doesn't date. He enjoys getting his dick wet with a different woman every night too much for a girlfriend."

The look of shock on her face is absolutely priceless. She whirls around and storms off. When I turn back to Jax, he's grinning like a Cheshire cat, biting his lip to stifle a laugh.

"You better hope your brother doesn't actually like her," he warns.

I roll my eyes. "Please. The moment she says 'girlfriend,' he'll skip the country. He's a total fuckboy who is into fake boobs and trashy women."

Broken

Jax raises an eyebrow. "You don't seem too fond of him."

I can't help but smile.

"He's my best friend. He's a good guy and a great brother but the man treats sex like therapy and his dick's the fucking shrink."

Jax pretends to be horrified. "Jesus. The mouth on you."

I shrug. "I can thank my brother for that."

He smirks, and a strange flutter stirs in my stomach. *What was that?*

"Anyway, I should get going. It was nice meeting you," I say, trying to shake off the feeling.

His smile dims a little, but he steps closer. "I'll wait with you until your Uber arrives." He pats the shoulder of a guy I hadn't noticed before—someone engrossed in conversation with a woman at the bar.

"I'm out. I'll call you tomorrow," Jax tells him. The guy barely glances up and waves him off.

Leaning in, Jax whispers, "My brother's a fuckboy too."

I laugh. Of all the things to have in common.

CHAPTER 3

Navigating through the bar has gotten trickier since I arrived. The place is packed now, making it feel claustrophobic and noisy. Jax places his hand on my lower back to guide me, and I flinch at the contact. He instantly removes it, and embarrassment washes over me. He probably thinks I'm still rattled from that bloody creep who got too close.

Broken

Stepping outside, the chilly air feels refreshing against my skin. Jax keeps a respectful distance, but I can't bring myself to meet his gaze. My eyes stay fixed on the ground as I dig my phone out of my pocket to check the Uber app.

"It'll be at least ten minutes," I mumble, my voice barely above a whisper. "Thanks for offering to wait, but you really don't have to."

He must think I'm a complete mess.

"What kind of gentleman would I be if I left you out here to fend for yourself?" his voice is deep and smooth, and it makes my heart race.

"Are you a gentleman?" I can't help but grin, still staring at my shoes.

"God, no. But I like to play pretend."

His laugh is so effortlessly charming that I finally look up, a goofy smile creeping across my face.

A taxi pulls up beside us, and three girls hop out, laughing and teetering in their heels. Jax keeps his gaze on me.

"Is the cab alright?" he asks.

Broken

I nod slowly, not wanting to break the spell he has over me—yet still feeling the pull to escape before I embarrass myself further. He waits for the last girl to climb out, then steps forward, holding the door open and motioning for me to hop in.

"Where do you live?" his voice is so mesmerising I nearly give away my address without thinking.

"That's a pretty personal question," I say with a smirk.

He chuckles. "I just need to know how much to give the driver."

Oh.

"That's very kind of you, but it's not necessary. It was lovely meeting you, Jax." I can't help but smile again.

He grins back, waiting for me to settle into the back seat before shutting the door. Then he opens the front and leans across the passenger side, handing the driver a fifty-dollar note.

"Hopefully that covers it."

I blink. *Did he seriously just do that?*

The driver glances at me. "Where to, love?"

Broken

"Um—right, Fairview Terrace."

Jax nods at the driver, who says, "Plenty."

"Keep the change," Jax adds with a wink in my direction.

"It was a pleasure to meet you, Ally."

He closes the door and steps back, slipping his hands into his pockets with a cheeky grin. I watch him as the taxi drives away, still in a daze.

Broken

CHAPTER 4

I had a dream about him last night. He wasn't doing much—just standing there with that delicious smirk.

I try to push him out of my mind during the day, but he's completely hijacked my brain. I catch myself staring blankly at my monitor, replaying our conversation, analysing his smile, wondering if he's thought about me at all today. It's ridiculous, of course —I know that. But try telling my subconscious. Even

Broken

worse, it's seeped into my draft. Suddenly, the main character—this brooding, pale vampire—has Jax's eyes, Jax's jawline, Jax's infuriatingly charming smirk. I actually had to stop reading because I was dissolving into a puddle of goo just imagining the character who now looked like Jax, and I had to laugh or I would've screamed.

This is going to make things interesting, to say the least.

By noon, I'm starving and frustrated after reading the same paragraph three times without absorbing a thing. I need greasy food, so I call across the street and order a burger and chips. I throw on some black yoga pants, an oversized black tee, and my new Chucks.

As I step out of my building, I hear Tyler's ringtone —'*The Bitch Song*' by Bowling for Soup—blaring from my back pocket. I can't resist starting the conversation by teasing him.

"I hear you're boyfriend material these days," I laugh.

"You're a fucking menace!" his words are stern, but his tone is playful.

Broken

"Can I be a bridesmaid?"

He snorts. "I have a feeling the bride doesn't like you very much."

"She said my shoes were hideous! She had it coming."

"Well, if I haven't already dropped her arse, I certainly would have for that comment."

Then I sense the shift in his tone.

"What the fuck were you thinking going out last night?"

Uh-oh. Dad voice: activated.

"Seriously, Banana! Don't think you're too old for me to drive down there and kick your sorry arse."

I hate that nickname, and he knows it. He's been calling me Banana since he was old enough to talk, and I've disliked it since I was old enough to talk back.

"Don't call me that. I thought you'd be cool with it since I was with your girlfriend," I sing-song, knowing it'll rile him up more.

"Do not fuck with me, kid! You know what? Fuck this! I'll be there in two hours."

Great. Now he's got my full attention.

Broken

I walk up to the burger shop and decide to eat in since it looks like I'll be on the phone for a while.

"No, really, I'm fine. I just thought it would be nice to have a normal night. But honestly, it was pretty boring."

Jax's face pops into my head—his smirk has me daydreaming again.

"BANANA!"

"What?"

"I asked which part wasn't boring?"

I can't tell him about the stunning man who's making it hard for me to focus—Ty would freak out.

"The part where your girlfriend confessed she's in love with you."

"Jesus. Moving right along... You sure you're alright?"

His concern makes my heart twitch. Tyler's been the only real family support I've had in years. My connection with my parents was never strong, but it completely vanished the moment I managed to escape their house.

They've always pointed fingers at me, claiming I

caused everything that happened that night and should take full responsibility. The toughest part was their demand for silence. They insisted I keep everything under wraps.

They said I'd already messed up Ty's life enough—why add to the family's shame by letting others know?

"I'm good."

"No nightmares?"

"None."

I decide to keep the other dream to myself—he'd be racing over before I could finish the sentence. It's also not worth stressing him out over the nightmare from a couple of nights ago. Jeanie mentioned that sometimes these things just happen for no reason and I shouldn't let it bother me.

I've already changed Ty's life enough—I don't want him worrying about me. When I told him I was leaving home, he tried to chain me to my bed, but he knew he was fighting a losing battle. I had to escape—I couldn't be that person anymore. Being there felt like being trapped. Every little thing reminded me of my past and the person I should've become. I was tormented not only by the memories but by the reality of what I'd never be. I had to get out, and Ty understood that.

"Thanks for the shoes, Ty. I really love them."

He exhales, and I can tell the storm has passed. We chat about random stuff for the next half hour. By the time I say goodbye and promise to call tomorrow, I feel lighter. Talking to him always lifts my spirits—but as soon as I set my phone down, Jax's smirk comes rushing back.

◆ ◆ ◆

I pick up a coffee for myself and one for Paul, the friendly concierge on the day shift. He's a great guy, probably in his sixties, with salt-and-pepper hair and a bit of a belly. He reminds me of my granddad with his dad jokes and warm smile. When I get to the lobby, Paul's not at his desk, so I leave his coffee there and make my way to the elevator.

Broken

It's nearly 2 PM, and I really need to dive into the vampire project to finish it before tomorrow. I've finished the book but still have seven chapters to edit.

The elevator dings as it reaches my floor, and the first thing that hits me is this sweet, floral scent. Not overpowering, but definitely noticeable. As I turn the corner into the hallway, I see that every door has a red rose with a little white tag in front of it.

What the hell?

All eight apartments—including mine—have a rose. I bend down to pick up the long-stemmed bloom and take a deep breath; I love flowers, and the classic rose scent is my favourite. The white tag is tied with a delicate string and has a florist's sticker on it. Flipping it over, I read seven simple words that leave me speechless:

It was a pleasure meeting you, Ally. J x.

I peek at my neighbour's door and notice their tag matches mine.

Did he really send one to every apartment? But how does he even know what floor I'm on? Maybe he sent them to everyone in the building? No—that's insane.

Broken

Could he have called the building to find out? That doesn't exactly fit with the whole security vibe here.

The rose is gorgeous—a deep crimson that practically vibrates. I have to thank the guy who sent it, Jax, but all I have is the florist's number. It's a short drive away, so he must be local. I hit call on the florist's site, feeling a mix of excitement and confusion.

Deep breath.

"Seeds and Stems, making the world a prettier place, one bloom at a time! How can I brighten your day?" The cheerful voice catches me off guard.

"Hi, I have a strange question. My name's Ally…"

"Oh my! He was hoping you'd call! I told him you'd be crazy not to, but he wasn't sure. He's a bit cold and detached, but the gesture is the sweetest I've seen in all my years!"

"You know Jax?"

"Met him this morning! I could tell he was a good one right away. He wanted pink or white, but I said, 'Absolutely not! Red is the way to a woman's heart!' If you want her to call you back, you need to go red. You know, most people go for mixed bouquets these days, but Jax? He's all about the single, perfect bloom. Says it makes a statement. And red is a bold statement. Like, I'm thinking of you, but with a bang! He thought his serious face would deter me, but I wasn't backing down."

"Look, I really appreciate your insights into Jax's floral philosophy, but I'm hoping to just thank him. Is there any chance you can give me his contact information?"

"Is that your dog I hear barking? I have three poodles, all rescues. Precious little angels. Anyway, back to Jax —"

Wow. This woman can really talk.

"Did he leave a contact number?" I ask, feeling a bit awkward. "You know, so I can thank him?"

"He definitely did. We usually keep personal info private, but I got his okay to share it when you called. I had a feeling you would ask, you know. Told him it was just a matter of time."

After ten minutes of awkward chit-chat—about what I look like, my feelings for Jax, when I WILL see him next, and how many kids I want—I finally hang up with his number in hand.

Now, I'm totally lost on what to do with it. Should I text or call? I really wish I had friends to help me figure this out. Calling seems better—texting feels too distant. But why can't my fingers just hit the call button? My hand is shaking like crazy.

Okay, texting it is. I don't have a nice vase for a single rose, so I grab an almost-empty wine bottle from the fridge, pour myself a glass (ignoring my no-drinking-before-three rule), and place the rose inside. I snap a pic and send it to him with a simple:

Ally: Thank you, J 🌹

He replies almost immediately:

Jax: You are very welcome, Ally.

Curiosity gets the better of me. I have to know how he knew what floor I was on. If I've left breadcrumbs on how to find me, I need to move and be more careful next time.

Ally: How did you know what floor I live on?

Jax: I didn't.

Ally: So what? Did you send a rose to every

apartment? lol, there must be 60 in the building.

Jax: 54, actually.

What the fuck?

Ally: I was joking!

Jax: I'm not. It's a huge building. So, how was the rest of your night? You made it home okay, I assume?

Ally: It was pretty quiet, thanks for asking.

After a few minutes of silence, I realise I'm not great at keeping the chat alive. I've been staring at the screen for ages, waiting for a reply, when suddenly a notification pops up.

Tyler: You were right. Ash just called to profess her love for me.

Ally: That's what you get for sticking your diseased cock in bimbos.

SHIT! SHIT! SHIT!

I didn't click on the notification to open it. I just told Jax he has a diseased dick.

FUCK.

Broken

He's going to think I'm more crazy than he already does. My cheeks are heating up, and I'm hit with this overwhelming wave of embarrassment as I scramble to figure out how to fix this mess. Thankfully, he replies almost immediately, just before I hit complete meltdown mode.

Jax: Bahahaha! I just spat coffee all over the
   desk from laughing obnoxiously loud
   during a work meeting. Been thinking about
   my cock, have you, Ally?

Ally: God, no. That wasn't meant for you. I am
   officially mortified.

Jax: I'm a bit let down by that. So, whose
   diseased cock are you thinking about?

I can't help but laugh. I wasn't picturing Jax naked before, but now I can't shake the thought. His chest was hard and warm when I touched him at the bar. What's that tattoo on his neck? Does it go down his arm or onto his chest? Where else might I find them?

Ally: That was meant for my brother! Not that I
   think about his—because that's just weird
   —but yeah, I'm going to go hide my head

Broken

in the oven now. Thanks again for the
rose and the cab last night.

Jax: Don't do that. Pretty people shouldn't be
hiding in the oven. Plus, I'm enjoying your
discomfort far too much. I was worried I
wouldn't hear from you.

Wait, he thinks I'm pretty? What do I even say to
that? *Umm, thanks*? No, that feels weird. We'll skip
over that comment—despite the butterflies fluttering
through my stomach.

Ally: After all the effort you put in, it'd be rude
not to thank you. But I'm a bit puzzled
why?

Jax: Because I want to know more about you.
But I was getting a serious fuck off vibe, so
I didn't dare ask for your number. I figured
out a way for you to ask for mine. ☺

Ally: Well played. Suddenly you're not so sure
of yourself, are you? What do you want to
know?

Jax: Will you have dinner with me?

Broken

I didn't see that coming. I've read his message three times and still can't seem to reply.

What I want to say and what I actually will say are totally different.

I'd love to be the girl who says yes, but I can't be that person. Jax seems funny, respectful, sweet—and hot as sin—but what do I really know about him?

My paranoia is screaming that he's dangerous.

All men are.

I lock my phone, set it aside, and grab my laptop to dive back into my safe—but suddenly dull—life.

Broken

CHAPTER 5

It's been two days, and I've started texting him only to delete my messages over and over again. I've built him up in my mind to an unrealistic level because, honestly, no one can be that good-looking.

I'm rereading our chat for the fourth time today, wondering if I would've acted differently if I'd known he would stick in my head like this. Would I have said yes to his dinner invite? It's hard to picture myself

Broken

agreeing, but daydreaming about a guy is new territory for me.

My phone buzzes with a message notification, but I don't rush to check it. It's been a couple of days since I last heard from Tyler, so I'm expecting something from him. Honestly, I don't get many messages from anyone else, so I'm pretty sure it's him reaching out. When I finally take a look at the screen ten minutes later, a wave of butterflies flutters in my stomach.

Jax: What's your favourite condiment?

What the fuck?

Surely, he messaged the wrong person—but it's an in to talk to him, so I'll take it.

Ally: Aioli. What about you?

Jax: Peanut butter.

Ally: That's not a condiment; that's a food.

Jax: It is too a condiment.

Ally: It's really not.

Jax: You spread it on food; therefore, it's a
condiment.

Ally: A condiment is something that enhances
the flavour of an existing food. Peanut

Broken

butter doesn't enhance anything—and it's just nasty!

This is not the conversation I was expecting. Are we really debating what food group peanut butter falls into?

Jax: Did you just Google the definition of a condiment? I'm not going to lie, I'm a little turned on right now.

Ally: You, sir, are one interesting individual! No, I didn't Google it—everyone knows what a condiment is.

Jax: Sir?? Well, I like the sound of that. Peanut butter enhances the flavour of everything; therefore, it's a condiment.

Ally: It most definitely is not—but why are we discussing condiments anyway?

Jax: Just a random topic to grab your attention. Clearly, it worked. Have a nice day, Ally

What just happened? Did he really message me to have a conversation about condiments? This incredibly beautiful man is an enigma.

Broken

◆ ◆ ◆

The following day, while having lunch, another message pops up on my phone. I can't help but smile, no matter how hard I try. I've had him on my mind all morning, and it's not just because he left me completely baffled—although that is definitely part of it.

His smirk keeps popping into my thoughts, and I can't shake it off. This morning, I went through my regular routine, but there was something different—I felt a bit lighter and couldn't stop smiling. What is it about this guy that's so fascinating?

Jax: What's your favourite curse word?

Ally: Cunt. And yours?

Jax: Jizzstain.

Ally: That's not a curse word.

Jax: Yes, it is!

Ally: It's an inappropriate combination of two
    non-curse words. Not a curse word.

Broken

Jax: Between my condiment preference and my choice of profanity, I'm really not winning at these conversations, am I?

Ally: That depends on how you measure success.

Jax: You responded, so I'll settle for winning the battle. Until tomorrow 😊

◆ ◆ ◆

The following day feels just like the last one. I find myself unable to shake thoughts of him as I sit here, anxiously waiting to hear from him. I hate this feeling. It's like a low hum of anxiety constantly buzzing just beneath the surface. My phone is practically glued to my hand, and I'm jumping at every notification, hoping it's Jax. Each time it's not, this little balloon of anticipation deflates inside me, leaving me feeling emptier than before.

I know, I know—I should just chill. But it's hard. I re-read our last messages a million times, trying to decipher some hidden meaning or predict when he might reply. I'm probably overthinking everything, but this waiting game is driving me crazy. I just wish he'd text already.

I need to distract myself, and my current script just isn't cutting it. Food. Food will distract me. While making a sandwich, my text alert sounds. I'm across the room faster than I thought possible, trying—and failing—to contain my smile.

Jax: What is your favourite simple pleasure?

Ally: Chocolate chip cookies. What's yours?

Jax: I'm afraid to answer. Experience tells me
you'll tell me my answer is wrong…

Ally: The last two questions required black-and-
white answers. This one operates in the
grey area. I don't think there is a wrong
answer.

Jax: Going to the gym.

Ally: FOR DUCKS SAKE! Turns out there is a
wrong answer. The gym is not a pleasure!

Jax: Ducks sake, haha. It is too! It's my second
favourite time of the day—I find it
therapeutic. Although, slight exaggeration

Broken

—I only go three times a week when I
come into the city for work.

Ally: Let me guess—seeing as you're a
masochist who enjoys the gym, I'm going
to guess your favourite would be your
alarm going off in the morning?

Jax: Nah, my favourite time is 12PM. Enjoy the
rest of your day 😊

That's a pretty exact time. Could it be his lunch break? It makes sense for him to message me when he's off the clock, but why not just mention it's lunch? I see it's 12:06 now, so he probably messaged me around noon. Scrolling back through the last few days of messages, I notice all the questions were sent at 12pm.

Cue the swooning.

◆ ◆ ◆

I'm doing my best to stay occupied today, just like I did yesterday, trying to ignore the ticking clock. I really want to dive deep into this book and lose myself

Broken

in its pages, but it's just not happening for me. *What if the particular bastard wasn't beautiful?* I could figure that out without even looking at the script—but in classic romance style, he still ends up with the girl. At least the typos and misplaced commas give me something to focus on.

By 12PM, I find myself staring at my phone, gripping it way too tightly. The minutes drag on, and I feel a wave of disappointment. Naturally, he's probably lost interest in this whole thing. Why would he want to text me when he could be with a real girl who's not scared to have dinner with him?

Jax: Sorry I'm late, my work meeting ran over.

What is something that strangers often incorrectly assume about you?

I'm feeling such a huge sense of relief. I didn't really notice how much he influenced my feelings until I felt let down by his silence. He's put the ball in my court, and it's up to me to take the initiative if I want to get to know him better.

Ally: That I'm confident and secure in myself.

And you? P.S. What do you do for work?

Broken

I've never really asked him anything that wasn't part of our usual back-and-forth, so I'm hoping he notices my attempt at an olive branch.

Jax: That I give up easily. Why, thank you for

asking, Ally— I'm an IT programmer 😊.

What do you do?

That actually made me laugh out loud. I don't fully grasp the joke, but it's still hilarious. There's no way this stunning guy—who hits the gym just for kicks—is a computer programmer. With those tattoos and that jawline, he's definitely more like a firefighter… or some kind of tradesman.

Ally: Haha! No, seriously—what do you do?

Jax: Ok, truth time. I'm a computer

programmer. Does that surprise you?

Ally: Well, yeah. You do not look like you work

in IT.

Jax: What do I look like I should do?

Be on the side of a bus in your damn underwear is the obvious answer here, but I haven't found that much confidence—so I'm going with my first assumption.

Ally: Fireman. Definitely a fireman.

Broken

Jax: Really? 😐

Ally: Don't be that guy. Surely you own a
    mirror.

Jax: Haha, I get this reaction a lot. Computers
    have always been something that came
    naturally to me, so it made sense. I'm a
    closeted nerd. You didn't tell me—how do
    you spend your days?

Ally: I arc-read books and line-edit them before
    they get self-published to online forums.

It's not a lie. He wanted to know how I fill my days,
and I gave him a straight answer. If I mention that I
don't have a 'real' job, it'll just lead to a bunch of
questions I'd rather avoid.

Jax: That's very cool! I'll have to start spell-
    checking my texts now that I know you're
    a grammar expert!

Jax: I'm heading into a working lunch. Same
    time tomorrow? =)

My mood takes a nosedive, knowing I have to wait
a whole 23 hours and 43 minutes to hear from him. Jax
is not only easy to talk to—he's fun as well. He makes

Broken

me feel warm and fuzzy inside. I was sure this feeling died years ago, and that I'd never get it back, certainly not from a man.

Broken

CHAPTER 6

The midday texts keep coming for the next three weeks, each one filled with Jax's random and puzzling questions. I'm having so much fun chatting with him that I barely notice how much I've shared about myself.

I'm too caught up in learning about him to remember to hold back.

He's 24, moved to Australia from the UK at age 7, has a fear of spiders, loves peanut butter on just about

Broken

anything (crunchy, not smooth), enjoys anime without shame, got suspended in high school for hacking the school's computer system just to prove he could, relies on three coffees a day, and struggles to sleep on days he doesn't go to the gym.

The more I find out about him, the more perplexed I become. What could he possibly gain from sending me these random questions every day at noon?

After a long day of tidying up and tackling laundry, I decide to pour out my mixed emotions about Jax in an email to Jeanie. I really want to have more conversations with him, but I'm stuck on how to approach it without putting myself in a position where I feel exposed or vulnerable. It's like I have this urge to connect, but the fear of letting my guard down makes it tricky to figure out the right way to start a deeper dialogue.

She's helped me navigate so many tough times that I know she'll be just as surprised by the tone of my email as I am while writing it.

I spend the rest of the evening with a book of my choosing and a glass of wine. I used to love a good sports romance, but it's been a while since one truly captivated me. Most of what I read for work is romance, which has drained the joy out of my downtime.

Plus, I had given up on the idea of a happy ending—people like me don't get that luxury. Yet lately, I've felt a flicker of hope.

My phone lights up, and while I roll my eyes at Tyler's persistent nature, I'm pleasantly surprised to see Jax's name pop up on my screen.

Jax: Sweet dreams, Ally x

Ally: Good night, Jax x

He's weightless above me, propped up on his elbows as his lips find their way to my neck. He teases with gentle sucks before trailing soft kisses up my jaw, locking eyes with me and murmurs, "Fuck, you're beautiful."

Suddenly, his lips crash into mine, the kiss filled with urgency as our tongues clash for control. He shifts his weight, his left hand exploring my chest

Broken

through my T-shirt. I push against his shoulder, urging him to sit back on his knees, and I follow suit.

I pull my shirt off and do the same to him, feeling the smoothness of his tanned skin under my fingers as I explore his chest and abs. He tangles his fingers in my hair, holding me steady while he claims my mouth again. As he loosens his grip, one hand caresses my cheek while the other moves to my back, unclipping my bra and sliding the straps down my arms.

When he breaks the kiss, I lean forward, chasing his lips, craving more. We're both panting, lost in the heat of the moment. His hands cup my breasts, fingers teasing the underside while his thumbs brush over my sensitive nipples. My back arches instinctively, a moan escaping before I can hold it back.

He bends down, taking one nipple into his mouth—sucking hard, then lightly biting—sending shivers through me as he rolls the other one between his fingers. I can feel pleasure building inside me.

He gently pushes me back down, his lips trailing down my stomach as his tongue circles my belly button, deftly undoing my jeans. Sitting between my

Broken

legs, he pulls them down, his gaze locked on the apex of my thighs before flashing that irresistible smirk as he lowers his face closer.

He looks hungry—starving to taste me—as he settles between my thighs and sets my legs over his shoulders.

The first swipe of his tongue against my sex has my back arching off the bed. His mouth is warm and slick as his tongue laps at me like I'm his favourite flavour of ice cream.

My hand grabs at his hair, pulling from the root, holding him in place against me. He backs off just long enough to run a finger through my wetness before sliding it inside.

His mouth closes around my clit and sucks while his finger curls, hitting a spot inside me that makes me see stars. The pleasure builds, pulling tight through my body like an overstretched elastic band.

His finger pumps into me as his tongue circles my clit.

"Jax, I'm so close."

His lips seal around my clit, sucking hard— and fireworks explode behind my closed eyes.

Broken

I jolt awake, heart racing and drenched in sweat, wondering what just happened. I've had my share of sex dreams, but never one like that.

There's a throbbing sensation between my thighs that makes my hand instinctively slip into my sleep shorts. I've never really been into self-pleasure—never quite figured out how to do it—but the pressure is too much to ignore.

My fingers glide through the slickness, finding that sweet spot that sends waves of pleasure through me. I experiment with different pressures and rhythms, but it only heightens the need.

I bring my other hand down, coating a finger with my own arousal before sliding it inside, still teasing my clit. It feels a bit awkward, but there's a warm buzz building inside me. It's not the explosive release I've read about, but it's definitely something new.

Images of Jax flood my mind—his smirk, those honey-coloured eyes—and I quicken my pace, desperate for more.

Broken

But just as I feel something starting to build, the sensation fades, leaving me hanging and frustrated. I slam my hands into the mattress and let out a groan of defeat.

After a few moments of sulking, I grab my phone and decide to text Jax, knowing full well this whole mess is somehow his fault—even if I'd never admit I just touched myself thinking about him.

Ally: Good morning

Jax: Good morning 😊

His reply comes through straight away, and my frustration takes the wheel. I type without thinking.

Ally: Would you like to have coffee with me?

Jax: I was starting to think you'd never ask 😊

What the fuck did I just do?

Broken

CHAPTER 7

I'm sitting on my bedroom floor, surrounded by a chaotic pile of clothes and shoes. I've changed outfits fifteen times, but nothing feels right. Meeting Jax for a drink after work seemed like a good idea—liquid courage and all—but I didn't expect the stress of getting ready for what might actually be a date. I'm so nervous I can barely sit still.

Plus, I need to tidy up before Tyler comes over tomorrow for his usual visit. I've always been a tidy

Broken

person, so he'll definitely know something's up if he sees my wardrobe exploded all over the floor.

I start sorting through the mess, putting away the definite nos and leaving a small maybe pile. My style is a bit quirky, but since Jax first met me in jeans, I decide to keep it simple—knee-length denim skirt, a fitted white top with cap sleeves that flatters my chest, pink glitter sneakers for a confidence boost, and a pearl hairband. My hair is sleek and straight, and I go for light, natural makeup.

The bar's only a short three-block stroll from here, and since it's still bright outside, I decide to walk, hoping the fresh air will help calm my jittery nerves.

I get there a little before six and debate whether to go inside or wait out front. Unsure of the dating etiquette, I choose to head in and order a drink—liquid courage and all that. The bar is cosy, with windows all around and plants in every corner, giving it a bit of a greenhouse vibe. Despite happy hour, the atmosphere is relaxed. I head to the bar and order a margarita with extra salt. I never drink hard liquor outside my house, but then again, I don't usually go out at night either. I guess I'm breaking all the rules tonight.

As I wait for the bartender to mix my drink, I can't shake the feeling that someone's watching me. That eerie sensation of being observed crawls up my spine, but I don't dare glance around. My gaze stays glued to the bar.

Suddenly, a figure appears on my left, and that velvety, smooth voice sends a shiver down my back.

"Fancy seeing you here."

My memory doesn't do him justice. Apparently, he can be that stunning. That lopsided grin of his makes my stomach flip like I've just swallowed a bag of butterflies.

"I was just in the neighbourhood," I squeak, cheeks heating in embarrassment.

I can't help checking him out—and wow, he looks amazing. When we met, it was jeans and a T-shirt, but today he's in a fitted light-grey suit that hugs his body just right. His broad shoulders fill out the jacket perfectly, tapering to slim hips where the button's fastened. The trousers hug his thighs snugly, and I

Broken

know I'm staring, but I can't stop. My eyes finally land on his face again, and that smirk is melting me.

To justify the ogling, I mumble something about being underdressed—as if that makes it okay to check him out from head to toe.

When my drink is ready, Jax grabs it and puts it on his tab, then gestures to a high table in the corner.

"I usually wear jeans and a T-shirt to work, but I had an important meeting today."

"Do you have a lot of important meetings?" I wonder silently if we can make a tradition of catching up after each one, just so I can see him in that suit again.

"Sure, all firemen do," he replies.

I choke on my margarita, and the jerk laughs. He gives me a pat on the back to help ease my coughing, but I tense at his touch. He must notice how stiff I've gotten because he quickly pulls his hand away, stepping back to give me space.

We chat for about an hour. Jax is effortlessly charming, cracking jokes while I stumble through safe topics. We're total opposites—he's laid-back and cool, and I'm a nervous fucking wreck—but somehow, he makes me feel comfortable. Safe, even.

I excuse myself to the bathroom, needing a moment away to catch my breath. As I wash my hands, I ponder how to end the night gracefully. I don't want it to end, but I know I need to take things slow. He's probably thinking about how to leave too but is too polite to say it.

When I return, there's a plate of chips with aioli and a glass of Gembrook Hill Sauvignon Blanc waiting for me.

My paranoid brain wonders how he knows my favourite wine, but I brush it off, too flattered to care.

He just shrugs at my smile. "Figured it was a safe bet—you sent a photo of the rose in the Gembrook Hill bottle, remember?"

This sweet, thoughtful man has completely disarmed me. I take a small step closer, before I can second-guess it. He gently tucks my hair behind my ear, and I don't flinch. Don't freeze. Don't retreat from the touch.

Broken

I'll no doubt spend hours later dissecting why with Jeanie, but right now I'm basking in the warmth of his presence and that intoxicating sandalwood scent.

After we polish off the chips and wine, Jax offers to order me an Uber while he settles the bill.

"I'm just going to walk."

"I'm going to have to insist on walking you home."

"Don't be silly, I don't live far."

"I know. I picked this place so you wouldn't have to travel, but I can't in good conscience let you walk home alone at night."

His slight frown makes me wonder if I'm inconveniencing him—or if he's worried I'll say no.

"It's part of my job as a fireman to keep the community safe," he adds with a serious tone.

My cheeks flush and I cover my face with my hands. "Seriously, you're never going to let that go, are you?"

"Not anytime soon." He smirks.

I convince myself it's purely for safety—not because I'm desperate to stretch out more time with him.

Broken

"Are you sure I'm not keeping you from anything?"

"There's nowhere I'd rather be."

My cheeks flush again as he lifts his hand and brushes the back of his knuckle against my cheek. When he steps back, I instantly miss the warmth, but I mask it and start walking.

He places a hand gently on my hip, and I flinch at the unexpected contact. But instead of pulling away, he gently steers me to the inside of the footpath, positioning himself between me and the road.

"Did you really just do that?" I ask, beaming.

"I did," he replies, walking beside me with his hands tucked in his pockets.

I fidget, folding my arms across my chest. Suddenly, Jax stops, unbuttons his jacket, and slips it off. He steps closer and drapes it over my shoulders, fastening the button again.

The scent of sandalwood surrounds me, and I close my eyes, breathing it in deeply. When I open them, he's watching me with a grin.

"You're really beautiful when you smile," he says softly.

Broken

I hadn't even realised I was smiling. I bite my bottom lip to hide it, and his gaze follows the motion. He clears his throat and steps back, gesturing for me to lead the way.

We walk in silence until we reach my building. I unbutton the jacket and slip it off, grateful for the scent lingering on my clothes as I hand it back.

"Thanks for tonight. I really had a nice time," I say, warmth bubbling in my chest.

He doesn't reply right away. When I look up, he's staring at my lips.

He steps closer, our bodies nearly touching, and tucks my hair behind my ear again, his fingers lingering. Tingles ripple across my skin. His eyes are locked on mine, searching.

Then he leans in, lips barely brushing mine. My hands find his chest instinctively, and his cradle my face. The kiss is soft, slow, savouring. His tongue teases the seam of my lips, and I part them without thinking.

Broken

His tongue slides against mine—unhurried, thorough, intoxicating. I've been kissed before, but never like this.

I tilt my head, deepening it, and his hand slips to my hip, pulling me closer. He nips playfully at my bottom lip and I gasp, heat pooling in my core.

He brushes his lips over mine one last time, then starts to pull back. I lean forward chasing his lips.

When I finally open my eyes, he's smiling—a real, full smile that lights up his face.

"I had a nice time too. Can I see you again?"

I can't find my voice, so I just nod.

He leans in for another soft kiss, then steps back.

I look down to avoid his gaze—but instead, I catch the unmistakable bulge in his suit pants.

He chuckles, catching my stare, and wipes the corner of his mouth with his thumb, looking adorably sheepish.

"Yep, that's my cue," he says with a grin.

I manage one last smile before practically sprinting into my building.

Broken

Looks like I'm diving back into the self-love journey tonight.

Broken

CHAPTER 8

My hormones are all over the place right now. I think it's because my period just started this morning, but honestly, I've never felt like this before.

When I got home from hanging out with Jax, I was so overheated I had to jump into a cold shower. It helped cool my skin down, but it didn't do anything to erase the vivid images of him that kept popping into my head—or the tingling sensations I can't seem to shake. I've been trying to tidy up my little two-bedroom apartment for the past hour, but I keep getting sidetracked by my thoughts. That kiss is lingering way longer than I expected. I can't stop thinking about how his tongue danced with mine, the taste of him, and that undeniable bulge. I find myself wondering what he looks like without any clothes on—but I quickly shut that thought down.

I really need to pull myself together before Ty arrives. Every other weekend since I moved here, Ty comes over to spend the night, and sometimes he brings his best friend Nate along—who's the only other man I trust completely. I've known Nate since he and Ty were in kindy together seventeen years ago, and he feels like the second sibling I never knew I wanted. He's just as protective as Ty, but in a more chilled-out way.

I wonder what Jax is doing right now... Nope, not going there.

Ty can be super observant when he wants to be, and he'll definitely pick up on something being off if I'm not careful. If he brings Nate this weekend, I'm really going to be in trouble.

I push all thoughts of Jax—and the cheeky message he sent me this morning—out of my mind and focus on changing the sheets in the spare room.

The Bitch Song starts playing, and I rush to answer it before it goes to voicemail.

"Hello, favourite brother!" I say, trying to keep it light.

"I'm your only brother," Ty replies.

"What the fuck am I, a duck?" I hear Nate's voice in the background, sounding a bit offended, and I realise this is going to be a long 24 hours. If Ty doesn't notice my spaced-out vibe, Nate definitely will.

"We just stopped for petrol about 20 minutes away. Need anything?" Ty asks.

"Yes. Tampons, please!"

Ty's groan makes me chuckle at his expense. This isn't the first time he's had to run out and grab tampons for me, but his reaction never fails to amuse me.

Broken

"She asked you for stoppers, didn't she?" Nate chimes in with a teasing tone, and I can almost picture Ty rolling his eyes in response.

"You're such a pussy. Don't worry, Banana, I got this. Mini, regular, or super?"

I have to fight the urge to tell Nate to drop the nickname since he's helping me out, but I really can't stand it.

"What the fuck? How do you even know that?" Ty sounds genuinely amused now.

"I'm a strong, independent white man in touch with my feminine side! That's how," Nate replies with a laugh.

"What does your feminine side have to do with anything? You don't need them, so why do you know so much about them?"

Honestly, these two bicker like an old married couple.

"Don't be such a pussy. A little blood never hurt anyone, and you should know that considering how much you love pussy."

Jesus, Nate!

Broken

"Regular, please!" I shout into the phone, desperate to end their ridiculous back-and-forth before hanging up.

◆ ◆ ◆

I can hear them approaching for a good thirty seconds before they finally step through the front door. Tyler's on my list of visitors and has a key, claiming it's for 'emergencies,' even though he lives a solid two hours away. He halts abruptly in the doorway, causing Nate to bump into him. Tyler's dark hair, with a hint of red—slightly darker than mine—is swept back off his face, his piercing green eyes assessing me.

"What the fuck, man?" Nate's dirty-blonde hair is now shorter than I remember, shaved on the sides and styled into a messy mohawk on top.

When he glances over at me, he must see what Tyler does, his gaze sweeping over me from head to toe.

God, I am so fucked.

Broken

"Hey guys, how was the drive?" I try to keep my tone casual, fighting the urge to shrink under their intense scrutiny.

"Why do you look different?" Ty asks, sounding more puzzled than angry.

A nervous laugh escapes me. "What? Don't be silly."

"You definitely look different," he insists—still not angry, but his gaze is making me uneasy.

I quickly throw out the only thing I think might make him uncomfortable enough to change the subject.

"Oh, it must be hormones from my period."

Tyler pretends to shudder in disgust but steps closer to me, leaving Nate still standing in the doorway, his eyes narrowed and fixed on my face.

Ty pulls me into a warm hug and plants a kiss on the top of my head. He's been my safe haven for the past few years, and his usual greeting brings me a sense of relief. As he releases me, I can't help but notice Nate still lingering at the door, studying me with his head cocked slightly to one side.

Broken

Ty pulls open the fridge and groans, "You could've warned us we were out of beer."

I'm too caught in a staring match with Nate to even notice he's speaking to me.

"Banana?"

"Shit, sorry. Yeah, you guys finished it last time you were here."

Nate finally strolls into the room and wraps me in a quick hug before turning to his best friend.

"I gotta take a piss, run down to the bottle-o across the street real quick. I'll set up the PlayStation."

Ty lets out a groan but heads toward the front door, leaving Nate to lean against the kitchen counter. The moment the door clicks shut, he's back to focusing on me.

"You going to tell me about it?"

I turn my back to him, trying to dodge his intense gaze, and start arranging the blanket fort in the living room where we'll be gaming for the next several hours.

"Tell you about what?" I shoot back.

Broken

"Whatever's got you looking so not broken," he replies, and I can't help but scoff, my annoyance clear on my face.

"Don't be like that, Banana, you know what I mean."

"DON'T CALL ME THAT!" I snap.

"I'm sorry, Ally."

"It's just hormones," I mutter.

"Maybe—but not in the way you're implying it," he counters.

"My own brother doesn't think anything of it, so why would you?"

"That man is blind to anything he doesn't want to see. Come on, what's going on?"

My phone buzzes on the counter, and I glance at it before quickly looking back at Nate. I don't have many friends, and the only other two people who text me are right here—which leaves Jax. Nate notices my distraction and follows my gaze.

"It's a guy, isn't it? Well, I'll be fucking damned!"

"You're wrong… and crazy… and so wrong."

A sly grin spreads across his face.

Broken

I'm so screwed.

He chuckles while shaking his head.

"Settle down, tiger. I won't tell the big, bad, overprotective wolf. Just be careful, yeah?"

I blew out a breath that had been locked in my chest. Honestly, things could've turned out way worse, and I'm a bit shocked they didn't. As I stroll into the kitchen, I can't help but wrap my arms around him, catching him off guard. Our relationship is one hundred percent platonic, and we don't usually get physical beyond the usual hellos.

Ty walks in and catches sight of us in a hug before I can pull away from Nate.

"What's happening here?" he asks, raising an eyebrow.

"Oh, nothing much. I'm just getting my fix since I haven't seen her in a month. So, what are we playing?"

❖ ❖ ❖

The rest of their time here goes by smoothly, and Tyler seems oblivious to me slipping into my room

Broken

every 20 minutes to text Jax. I really appreciate Nate for keeping him occupied during that time.

As they're about to leave the following day, Nate gives me a hug at the front door and reminds me to be careful—but luckily, Tyler doesn't catch on to the underlying meaning behind his words. I've never been so relieved to walk them to their car and watch them drive away.

CHAPTER 9

Jax keeps firing off random questions every day at noon, no matter what we're chatting about in our text thread.

It's been nearly a month since he started the question game, and he still seems totally into our little back-and-forth. No matter the topic, the questions pop up and slide seamlessly into the conversation.

Broken

Still, I can't shake the thought—how many other women might be caught up in the same game with him?

The other night, I turned down his dinner invite and suggested we meet up on Friday instead. Now that Friday afternoon is here, I'm feeling a mix of nerves and excitement, just like last time.

He's reserved a table at that Italian place just a short stroll from my apartment, and I can't help but feel a little giddy about how thoughtful he is as I make my way there.

Time slips by, and what feels like minutes turns into three hours. I'm completely at ease, smiling the whole way through dinner.

Jax has this way of making me feel safe and grounded. I've been so shut off for so long that I'd almost forgotten what it felt like to just be me. Somehow, Jax helps me rediscover myself—even when I didn't realise I'd been lost.

With him, I don't have to pretend. I can just be. And it's refreshing.

Broken

As we walk back to my place, he takes my hand, and the warmth of his skin sends a delightful tingle up my arm.

But as we approach my building, a wave of disappointment hits me. I realise I'm not ready for the night to end.

"What's wrong?" he asks, his voice laced with genuine concern.

I try to hide behind a bright smile, but he sees through it.

"I was just thinking… I'm not ready for the night to end," I admit, surprised by my own boldness, my voice tinged with vulnerability.

His smile lights up his whole face.

"It doesn't have to end yet. Want to go for a drink?"

The thought of this thoughtful, charming man wanting to spend more time with me sends my heart racing. I feel a surge of something bold, letting myself lean into the moment.

"Would you like to come up for a drink?" I ask. I'm shocked by my own confidence—but I don't regret it.

Broken

He gently cups my face and leans in, kissing me with an urgency that ignites something deep inside. The kiss is electric. I pull him closer, my hands clutching his shirt.

I brace for the familiar fear to creep in—but it doesn't.

"Are you sure?" he murmurs. His scent, the sound of his voice, the way he fills the space—it all leaves me dizzy with want.

I simply nod, afraid if I speak, my voice will betray me.

As we walk to the elevator, he holds my hand, warmth radiating from him.

But when we reach my door, nerves take over. I fumble with my keys, dropping them like a klutz.

Jax bends down to pick them up, handing them to me with a soft smile.

My hands tremble. He notices but is too polite to mention it. Instead, his fingers trail from the keys to my wrist, tracing soft circles with his thumb—a small gesture that calms me just enough.

I can do this.

Broken

Inside, my apartment looks different. Maybe it's just because he's here, but somehow, he fits.

I'm not used to sharing my space with anyone besides Tyler and Nate, but surprisingly, it doesn't feel weird.

As I take off my jacket and drape it over the back of the couch, he steps forward, his hands finding my hips when I turn around.

That smirk of his makes me forget all about offering him a drink. Instead, I step closer, rising on tiptoes to kiss him.

His fingers tangle in my hair, anchoring me as he kisses me back with equal intensity.

His tongue dances with mine, sending a rush through me, making my thighs clench, igniting a fire in my core.

His woodsy scent makes my head spin.

He shifts, pulling me with him, pressing me against the wall.

His lips trail from my mouth down to my neck, drawing a moan from my lips.

"God, Ally, you're so beautiful," he murmurs, and his words send a shiver across my skin.

Broken

I feel the heat flood my body, desire pooling between my legs.

He takes my hands—still gripping his shirt—and pins them above my head, bringing our bodies flush.

The friction of my breasts against his chest hardens my nipples.

He kisses me again, breath-stealing and full of hunger.

But then his hand slides down to my thigh, and I freeze.

The wall at my back. His weight against me. His fingers on my leg.

I'm no longer here.

A tidal wave of panic crashes into me—so sudden and intense I can't breathe or think. I react on instinct.

My free hand shoves hard against his chest. He stumbles back.

I gasp for air, eyes squeezed shut.

When I manage to open them, everything feels off.

There's no beach, no salt in the air. No car park. No night-time shadows.

Broken

Just my apartment.

White walls. Timber tiles. My furniture. My laptop on the kitchen counter.

And Jax, standing in the middle of it all, looking confused but not angry.

"I… I'm sorry. I panicked," I manage, voice shaky.

"Why did you panic?" he asks gently, like he's speaking to a frightened animal.

I can't answer. The words don't come.

After a long pause, he tries again.

"Ally, why did you panic?"

He stays where he is, leaning on the back of the couch, giving me space. I'm grateful.

I stare at the floor, unable to meet his eyes, terrified I'll see disgust or pity staring back. I've seen it before. From old friends. From strangers who'd heard the rumours. But I can't stomach it from him. Not him.

"Who touched you without permission?" His words jolt me. Panic rises again.

But he's still there. Calm. Steady. He's not running.

"You froze with that jackass at the bar. You flinch when I get too close. And just now, you all but assaulted me for even thinking about touching you. It's a fair assumption."

"That was barely assault. And I like it when you touch me," I blurt, mortified.

What the fuck is wrong with me?

He chuckles, tension easing. He takes a careful step closer, palms raised in peace, and gently tucks a strand of hair behind my ear.

"Ally, I can't know where the boundaries are if I don't understand them."

He's Perfect.

He knows the bombshell that's coming and he responds with the most perfect thing he could say.

I lean into his touch, inhaling the warm scent of sandalwood.

"A guy from school. I was 16," I whisper. It's not much, but it's a start.

He doesn't push. Just brushes his fingertips along my scalp.

"I'm sorry. Can we move away from the wall?" I blurt.

Broken

He looks at the wall, confused, but says nothing. He takes my hand and leads me to the couch.

I hesitate. "Would you like a drink? I'd like a drink. I'm going to *need* a drink."

"Sure. Anything you've got."

I'm glad Ty and Nate didn't finish off the beers but I will need to replace them before next weekend. They'd give me hell if they found out I had a guy over.

I grab a beer for Jax, pour myself a large glass of wine, then take a bold swig straight from my emergency bottle of tequila.

The burn makes me wince. I glance at Jax, expecting judgement—but he just looks amused.

I return to the couch, unsure where to sit. He gestures beside him.

I perch there, awkward. He drapes an arm over the back of the couch—not too close, not too far.

"His sister used to date my brother. We hung out a lot. He always said he liked me, but I thought it was just a crush."

"Can't imagine your overprotective brother liked that much."

Broken

"He wasn't protective back then," I say, eyes fixed on my lap.

Silence.

"Did he touch you?" he asks softly. I nod.

"Did he make you touch him?" Another nod.

"Has anyone else touched you since?"

I shake my head.

"Ally… are you a virgin?"

"No," I say too quickly. I sound pathetic, but I need to move this along.

"My boyfriend at the time noticed I was missing and came to find me. My brother nearly beat him to death before his friend pulled him off."

"I think I like your brother," Jax says.

I cant help but snort, "Don't get too attached. He wouldn't like you."

"Can't say I'd blame him."

"If you want to leave, I get it."

I hear the beer bottle clink as he sets it down. He lifts my chin with a knuckle, forcing me to meet his gaze.

Broken

"I'm not going anywhere. Not unless you ask me to."

I shake my head, just slightly.

He grins.

The scent of him. The gentleness in his touch. The way he gets me.

And somehow, after everything I've shared, he still wants to stay.

Broken

CHAPTER 10

I wake up with a heavy weight on my chest. I opened up to Jax. We spent an hour just cuddling on the couch, occasionally kissing, but he didn't try to make any further moves, and honestly, I can't fault him for that. He mentioned wanting to see me again, but deep down, I have this nagging feeling that in the light of day, he will change his mind.

Broken

Everything seems so different in the daylight, and now that I've had some time to think, I realise he probably won't want to deal with the emotional baggage I bring along. It stings to accept that, but I can't be upset with him. Starting something physical with me would definitely be a complicated mess. I'm frustrated with myself for taking so long to get to this point; if I hadn't been so afraid in the past, I might have been better equipped to dive into a relationship with Jax.

I send off a frantic SOS to Jeanie, filling her in on everything that happened last night—complete with my panic attack—desperately seeking her advice. I can't help but wonder if I'll always react like this or if it's just because it was the first time I let someone get close enough to really make me feel vulnerable. I'm also really struggling with this overwhelming feeling of insecurity about Jax not wanting to see me again. I can't shake the thought that maybe he just doesn't see me the same way anymore, and that uncertainty is really hard to deal with. I know she'll probably say there's no manual for situations like this. That I should

Broken

visualise the end goal of where I want to be in five years to set realistic goals to get there, but sharing my jumbled thoughts with her always brings me some clarity.

Just as I'm stepping out of the shower, my phone buzzes with a message.

> **Jax**: Good morning, beautiful. How are you feeling this morning?
>
> **Ally**: Good morning. Good, thank you. More importantly, how are you?
>
> **Jax**: Honestly, I'm angry at the world, but I think I can tame it by fighting a few fires 😊
>
> **Ally**: Really? More fireman jokes?
>
> **Jax**: Always. Do you have any plans for tonight?
>
> **Ally**: No. What did you have in mind?
>
> **Jax**: How about dinner at my place? I can't cook for shit, but I'm a pro at ordering takeaway.
>
> **Ally**: That sounds nice.
>
> **Jax**: It's a date. See you at 6!

Broken

A huge smile spreads across my face. Maybe he really can handle all of me after all.

◆ ◆ ◆

I spent the rest of my day, including the half-hour drive to Jax's place, mulling over my choices. I really like this guy, and the thought of a physical relationship with him excites me, but I know I need to get over that initial hurdle first. Honestly, I've imagined his hands on my body more times than I can count, picturing what it would feel like to have him close—against me, beneath me, and even inside me. Just thinking about it sends heat through my skin and makes me feel all tingly.

I've been struggling to figure out how to give myself the kind of relief I crave, so I finally decided to take a leap and ordered a vibrator today. It won't arrive for another four days, but it's something I never thought I needed, until I met Jax. I guess that means I'm not completely broken after all.

Broken

As I turn down the street to the address he sent me, I can't shake the feeling that I might have gotten it wrong. The neighbourhood looks so suburban, filled with trees and kids playing outside, which is nothing like what I expected from him. I pull up to the address, feeling a bit confused because it's a townhouse?

I had pictured him living in an apartment like mine, but this two-storey place gives off some serious adult vibes. I park on the street and step out of the car, nerves bubbling up inside me. There's this weird sensation that creeps up the back of my neck, making me feel like I'm being watched. My mind, always ready to spin out, runs wild with paranoia, especially when I'm feeling doubtful. But if he truly didn't want to see me again, he wouldn't have gone out of his way to invite me over, would he?

When he opens the door, that familiar smirk is plastered on his face, his hair damp and sticking up in all directions—and oh my goodness, he's shirtless. There is a god, and clearly, she's a woman for creating someone as stunning as Jax. His full sleeve tattoo flows down his arm and across the left side of his chest

Broken

in a mix of swirls and patterns that look almost tribal but with a more relaxed vibe, ending just above some seriously lickable abs. They're not overly defined, but there's enough there to count—six, definitely six—and I can't help but stare shamelessly at his body.

He clears his throat, and I glance up to see his face still wearing that cheeky smirk, eyebrows raised in playful mischief.

Busted!

He chuckles, shaking his head, and asks, "Are you going to come in, or are you just going to stand there and objectify me all night?"

A nervous laugh slips out before I can catch myself, and I quickly mumble, "Sorry."

"Make yourself at home; I'll just grab a shirt," he calls over his shoulder as he bounds up the stairs with ease.

Oh no, please don't do that!

I step further into the room, taking in the surroundings. The space is open and airy, with crisp white walls, sleek black furniture, and touches of dark green in the decor. My eyes are drawn to a collection of framed photos on the end table behind the couch: pictures of him with what I assume are his parents; a childhood shot with his brother in matching soccer uniforms; a recent family photo of the four of them; and a quirky anime graphic that makes me chuckle. It's hard not to notice, though, that Jax doesn't seem to be smiling in any of those pictures.

"Don't be making fun of the classics," he says from behind me, and I turn around, slightly let down, to see him already dressed.

He strides right into my personal space and kisses me with urgency. I can't help but notice how different he feels from the guy who was so gentle with me last night. His fingers weave through my hair, his tongue dances with mine, and his intoxicating scent envelops me. I'm completely lost in the moment. He pulls away too soon, taking my hand and leading me to the kitchen, stopping in front of a high stool tucked under a sleek kitchen bar.

"Make yourself comfortable; I'll grab you a drink."

Broken

It's funny how I've barely spoken since I got here, yet there's this unexpected ease between us after what happened last night.

He opens a cabinet and pulls out two wine glasses, then heads to the fridge for a bottle of Gembrook Hill Sauvignon Blanc. I feel a rush of warmth at his thoughtfulness as he places a glass in front of me and leans casually against the kitchen bar beside my seat. I take a sip, and the familiar flavour dances on my palate, reminding me of how much effort he's put into making me feel comfortable.

My legs move of their own accord, and I find myself standing in front of him, leaning in and pulling his lips down to meet mine. He hesitates for just a moment, then sets his glass aside and wraps his arms around me, pulling me close. His kiss is back to being gentle and restrained, and it frustrates me because it's nothing like the passionate kiss we shared moments ago. I want more, so I deepen the kiss and run my fingers along the back of his neck, urging him to let go.

He breaks away, his lips trailing down to my neck, kissing and teasing my sensitive skin, sending shivers

Broken

through me. My breath quickens. Need builds inside me, spilling out before I even think to stop it.

"Touch me," I whisper, completely lost in the moment and no longer in control of my desires. He pulls back slightly, uncertainty flickering in his eyes.

"Please, Jax, I need you to touch me."

His gaze flickers back and forth between my eyes, weighing whether I'm being genuine or if I'm about to go into meltdown again.

"Keep your eyes on me. Don't close them."

I give a tense nod, but he immediately shakes his head. "Use your words."

"I won't close my eyes," I insist.

His hands find their way to my hips, applying a gentle squeeze while his thumbs move in a soothing rhythm. He shifts his gaze between my eyes, searching for any sign of doubt or fear, but there's nothing of the sort. I feel safe. Grounded. His response to what I shared with him last night has only intensified my feelings for him and made me feel more secure. Now, all I can focus on is him.

Broken

His fingers gradually travel to the centre of my lower stomach, brushing against the waistline of my knee-length skirt. The drawn-out moment starts to make me feel a bit self-conscious, almost like we're following a script instead of being in the moment. I pull my hands away from his neck and reach for the zip at the back of my skirt, letting it slide down until the fabric pools around my ankles.

He trails a finger down the front of my panties, and I gasp, instinctively shutting my eyes.

"Eyes on me," he commands in a low, gravelly voice, and I quickly open them again. He wants me to stay present, to know it's him touching me rather than getting lost in my thoughts.

As his middle finger glides along my sex, a moan escapes my lips, prompting him to repeat the motion. His gaze is intense, locked onto mine as he slips his finger inside the edge of my panties, and the sharp intake of breath I take brings a wicked smirk to his face.

"You're so wet for me," he whispers.

Broken

At that moment, my mind goes blank; all I can think about is his touch. He slides his finger through my arousal, circling my clit, and my knees buckle beneath me. His other hand remains firmly on my hip as my head falls against his chest.

He chuckles softly, repeating the motion, and I feel my entire body tense in response.

"Stay with me," he says again, his voice low and commanding, and honestly, I can't get enough of it. There's this rush of excitement that washes over me from his instruction. I tilt my head back to meet his gaze, and his eyes are filled with a wild hunger that makes my heart race. I can just tell he'd consume me whole if he had the chance.

His finger traces around my entrance before sliding inside, and I wince a little. It's not exactly painful, but the stretch is definitely uncomfortable at first as he retracts his finger.

"Fuck, you're tight. Nice and slow, beautiful, I won't hurt you," he murmurs.

Broken

With just the tip of his finger, he eases in and out, gradually stretching me until that initial discomfort melts into something far more pleasurable.

"Are you okay?" he checks in.

I can barely manage to respond, my voice trembling with need as I plead, "Don't stop, please."

He slides his finger in deep and curls it just right while his thumb finds my clit, teasing it in tight circles that send waves of sensation through me until I'm clenching around him.

"Let go," he whispers, his voice sultry against my ear, and suddenly, I'm exploding. My core tightens around his finger, and my leg quakes as a rush of tingles courses through me, leaving me gasping and clutching at his shirt. It's unlike anything I've ever felt before—my entire body igniting with pleasure—and I'm torn between wanting it to end and wishing it would last forever. I rest my forehead against his chest, trying to catch my breath, my mind swirling as I slowly come back to reality.

Wow. So that's what that feels like.

Shit. Did I say that out loud?

Broken

Jax pulls his finger away, and I can't help but feel a sudden emptiness where the pressure used to be. He tilts my chin up, making me meet his gaze, and I can see the amusement dancing in his eyes.

"Was that your first orgasm?" he teases.

I groan, mortified that I actually blurted that information out. I try to fight against his finger holding me hostage, wanting to hide away from his amusement.

"I didn't mean to say that," I mumble, feeling the heat radiate from my cheeks.

He just chuckles softly, wrapping his arms around me, pulling me closer, and plants a gentle kiss on the top of my head, making me feel both embarrassed and oddly comforted.

And strangely... okay.

Broken

CHAPTER 11

We spend a couple of hours just hanging out in his living room, eating Chinese takeaway and chatting about random stuff that doesn't really matter. He mentions that he often works from home, which is why he enjoys the suburban feel more than the hustle and bustle of the city.

When he starts asking about my job, I quickly shift gears and ask him to show me his workspace instead. He leads me upstairs to the second floor, where all the doors are wide open, revealing two bedrooms and a bathroom. Everything has that lived-in charm but is still neat and organised, and I find myself slowing down as I pass his bedroom, curious about what it would be like to be there with him. A blush creeps up my neck just as he turns to see what's caught my attention, following my gaze to the bed. He shoots me a playful smirk and gives my hand a gentle tug, leading me to the end of the hall to the second bedroom, where his workspace is set up. There are three monitors on a desk, each with a keyboard in front, plus two laptops off to the side.

"Wow!" I'm still struggling to align Jax with what he does for a living — he's too beautiful to hide behind a computer, let alone be good at them.

"Not what you expect?"

"You're not what I expected. Aren't computer guys supposed to be geeky?"

He chuckles softly. "I'm definitely a geek; I just haven't shown you that side of me yet."

As I glance around the room, I notice a massive glass cabinet filled with four tiers of anime figures I've

Broken

never encountered before. The walls are adorned with framed illustrations from various comic strips, and an oversized straw hat casually rests on the back of a computer chair, hanging by a string.

"I'm starting to see that," I say, feeling him approach from behind. He places his hands on my hips, turning me into him, and I instinctively wrap my arms around the back of his neck. Our lips meet in a soft, tentative kiss that quickly escalates into something more passionate.

Feeling bold, I let my hands wander down his body, pausing on his chest before continuing down to his stomach, lifting his T-shirt to explore his warm, firm skin. My fingers glide back and forth, making his stomach clench.

I venture lower, my palm brushing against the noticeable bulge in his jeans, and I instinctively curl my fingers around it, causing a deep groan to escape his lips. The sound sends a thrill through me; I've never intentionally made a man groan before, and I'm curious about what other reactions I can draw from him—how he would look when he's completely undone.

I fumble with the button on his jeans, finally managing to pop it open and slide the zip down. His forehead rests against mine, his breath quickening, eyes shut tight.

"Eyes on me," I tease, and he chuckles, but his gaze locks onto mine.

"Do you want to stop?" he asks, and I reply with a firm "No," as I slip my hand into the front of his fitted boxers.

"Thank god!" he hisses as I make contact, wrapping my hand around his impressive length. There isn't much space to manoeuvre, and just as I'm trying to figure out how to get his pants off while still looking alluring, the doorbell rings. Almost immediately, a loud, slurred voice calls out, "Jax, I love you!"

His head falls onto my shoulder, and he lets out a groan that sounds like pure agony.

"For fuck's sake!" he exclaims, quickly adjusting himself by tucking his erection into the waistband of his boxers, making it stick out just enough to be noticeable, and I find myself unable to look away. The tip glistens with a bead of moisture, and I have an overwhelming urge to taste it. He quickly fixes his appearance by buttoning up his jeans and pulling his shirt down to conceal himself more effectively. Then, he grabs my hand and guides me down the stairs. Once we reach the bottom, he lets go of my hand and goes to open the front door.

"JACKSON! WHERE HAVE YOU BEEN ALL MY LIFE?" his brother—who I recognise from the night we met at the bar—shouts, his voice booming through the house. Jax grabs him by the wrist, pulling his drunken arse inside.

"Jesus, you're handsy. Still not getting any?" I stand frozen, embarrassment washing over me as my face and neck turn crimson. Jax runs a hand down his face, groaning in frustration. He shoots his brother a glare that could melt steel and asks, "What are you doing here?"

But his brother doesn't respond; he's too busy noticing me standing at the bottom of the stairs—undoubtedly as red as a ripe tomato.

Broken

"So, you're the reason my brother blew me off tonight? A pleasure to meet you, darling. I'm Oliver, Jax's older and marginally more charming brother," he says with a playful wink.

Now, I won't deny that Oliver has his charm—he isn't hard on the eyes by any means—but I wouldn't go as far as to say he's better looking than Jax. His hair is a bit longer on the sides, and he has a more solid build, but he lacks Jax's striking features and that warm, inviting vibe that makes me feel safe.

"That still doesn't explain why you're here, arsehole," Jax snaps, clearly irritated as he steps in front of me, positioning himself protectively between me and his brother. Oliver, however, seems unfazed by Jax's anger; he leans slightly to the side, trying to get a better look at me, like he's trying to figure me out. He clicks his tongue, as if I'm some kind of riddle he needs to solve.

"Where were you tonight? It's not even ten, and you're white-girl wasted," Jax asks.

"Just at your local pub," Oliver replies. He's making me feel a bit uneasy under his intense gaze.

Broken

"So that's why you're here. You've fucked through that place too many times and didn't find anything new to hold your interest," Jax teases, clearly enjoying the chance to poke fun at his brother.

Oliver's attention snaps back to Jax, and he shoots him a glare. "That's rich coming from the guy who fucked every girl in our high school."

Jax freezes, his posture stiffening as I see the muscles in his back tense up, clearly not pleased with that jab.

"Alright, Oli, you have to go." Jax says, giving his brother a firm nudge towards the door.

"What? Why?"

I finally manage to speak up, my throat feeling tight.

"Actually, I think I should be going," I say, feeling a strange tension in the air that makes me want to distance myself from Jax as quickly as possible.

I hurry past them, slipping on my shoes in a rush before Jax can catch up. I grab my jacket from the couch, throwing it over my arm instead of putting it on properly to save time. As I turn to make my way to the door, I bump into Jax, who steadies me with a gentle grip on my arm, sending a familiar shiver down my spine.

"Please don't go," he says softly, his tone almost pleading, as if he understands my urge to flee even better than I do.

"It's getting late," I reply, avoiding his gaze because I'm scared of what I might see in his eyes. He lets out a sigh of resignation and offers, "I'll walk you to your car."

"No!" I blurt out, the urgency to escape overwhelming my better judgement. I quickly soften my tone. "I mean, it's really not necessary. Just stay with your brother." I make a beeline for the door, brushing past Oli.

"It was nice to meet you. Good luck finding new girls to fuck," I throw over my shoulder with a hint of sarcasm, but he just chuckles.

Ignoring my attempt to leave, Jax follows me outside and grabs my elbow before I can open the door.

"Don't leave like this," he urges.

"What do you mean?"

Broken

He gently lifts my chin with his knuckle, forcing me to meet his gaze. "He's drunk; don't take what he says seriously," he says, sounding a bit irritated, but I can't tell if it's directed at his brother or my hasty exit.

"But is it true?" I challenge, and he shoves his hands into his jeans pockets, looking a bit sheepish.

"Not all of them."

"But the majority?" I find myself asking, even though I really don't want to know the number of women he's been with. Just thinking about it makes me feel so inadequate, and I know that putting a figure on it would only amplify my insecurities.

His jaw tightens, and he seems deep in thought, weighing how much to share with me.

"A guy in my year and I used to compete to see who could get more girls," he admits.

A wave of anger surges through me, and I ball my fists at my sides to keep from lashing out at him. This amazing, thoughtful guy turned women into mere points in a game?

"Are you serious? You treat sex like it's some kind of sport? What am I, just a challenge?"

Broken

"What? No. Of course not," he says, but his words lack conviction.

"I can't do this," I say, cutting him off.

He tries to say something, but I'm already in my car, slamming the door shut before he can finish his sentence. As I drive away from his place, tears start to spill down my cheeks, and I can't help but feel like such a fool.

CHAPTER 12

*T*he *Bitch song* blaring on repeat jolts me awake the next morning, after I finally managed to drift off around 4AM.

"Hey."

"Are you still asleep? What's wrong?"

"Nothing's wrong; why do you think that?" I reply, a bit defensively.

"Because you can't sleep past 8 unless you're sick or…" he trails off, clearly hesitant to finish that thought.

Broken

"Broken?" I suggest, knowing that's the unofficial term for when I'm so deep in depression I can't even get out of bed. When he doesn't say anything, I rush to fill the gap.

"I'm not sick or broken, arsehole. I just stayed up late reading a draft. I couldn't put the damn thing down," I admit, irritation creeping into my tone.

"Do you want me to come down?" His concern makes me feel guilty for snapping at him.

"No, I'm sorry. I'm just tired. I'm fine, really. I just went to bed late."

As I hold the phone to my ear, a message alert pings, but I ignore it to focus on Ty. We chat for about twenty minutes, and I try not to dwell on the message waiting for me. Since meeting Jax a month ago, I've received a ton of messages from him, and I still get butterflies every time his name pops up on my screen. I finally come up with a reason to end the conversation with Ty and quickly grab my laptop to shoot an email to Jeanie before Jax's message has a chance to muddle my feelings further.

Broken

I open up to her about how I stepped out of my comfort zone regarding physical intimacy, and my concerns about what I learnt about Jax last night. I'm really crossing my fingers that she'll be supportive and understand my desire to get involved with someone who has a past like his. My own history is already fucked up, and I really don't want to complicate things further by adding his attitude towards sex into the equation.

I don't wait for her response before clicking on the message, my stomach twisting in knots.

Jax: What's the stupidest thing you ever did?

He wants to play that message game? I guess we never really stopped, since I still get a question from him every day at noon, but they always seem to float outside the usual flow of our conversation.

Against my better judgement, I find myself typing a reply.

Ally: When I was 9, I fell out of a tree I was
warned not to climb repeatedly and ended
up breaking my wrist. What about you?
Jax: Not telling you what a scumbag I used to

Broken

be.

Ally: Used to be?

Jax: I was a dumb kid chasing after quick
thrills. I've grown up a lot in the past six
years. I now understand the value of
physical intimacy.

I struggle to connect the Jax I've gotten to know
with the one he and his brother painted last night, but I
can't shake this uneasy feeling about him fucking his
way through school. Maybe he's turned a new leaf,
though; I know I'm not the same person I was a few
years back. The difference is that I didn't exactly
evolve for the better—but who's to say he hasn't?

Just as I'm mulling over how to respond, another
message pops up.

Jax: Have dinner with me?

I really should just say no, and deep down I know
that. But I can't help seriously thinking about his offer.
Over the weeks I've known Jax, he's somehow
managed to start piecing me back together. He sees me
for who I am — imperfections and all — and still
genuinely wants to spend time with me. His kindness,

Broken

thoughtfulness, and patience are game-changing. It wouldn't be fair for me to hold his past against him, especially when he's been so understanding about mine.

Ally: Ok.

◆ ◆ ◆

Jax is waiting for me outside my apartment building, but to my disappointment, he makes no move to kiss me. All day, I've told myself to stay grounded, to maintain some emotional distance, but the moment I catch a whiff of his scent, I lean closer without thinking. My hands instinctively find his chest, and before I know it, I'm pulling him down to meet my lips. His kiss is soft, yet it sets off a fire in me—I dig my nails into his neck and tease his bottom lip with my tongue. He groans low in his throat, gripping my hips tightly enough that I wonder if he'll leave marks before pulling me even closer.

"I missed you," he murmurs, voice rough.

Broken

"You saw me last night," I reply, surprised by the unexpected neediness in my words.

"Still missed you." He presses a quick kiss to my lips, then steps back and takes my hand, leading me to his car.

The drive to dinner is wrapped in a quiet tension. That kiss may have melted the physical edge, but something unspoken still hangs between us. I lace my fingers with his and place his hand on my thigh, hoping to smooth out the awkwardness. When I glance over, his smile makes my shoulders relax.

"So, what's for dinner?"

"Well, we've had Italian and Chinese recently, so I was thinking Japanese. You like sushi?"

"I love sushi."

"There's this great place near my work. Their cocktails are amazing too."

"Oh, I don't really do hard liquor."

He chuckles. "What do you call tequila?"

"I usually only drink at home—unless I really need the liquid courage. Even then, just one drink."

Broken

He squeezes my hand. "I promise I'll keep you safe."

His words, so simple and casual, ground me. I sink deeper into the seat, feeling unexpectedly secure in his presence.

I believe him.

Dinner is easy and light, full of laughter and the kind of conversation that makes time feel irrelevant. Jax has this uncanny ability to draw out the version of me that existed before everything fell apart—the version I thought was gone. No matter how hard I try to keep my guard up, he slips through, effortless. Everything about him feels intuitive, like he's following a script written just for me.

I end up ordering a cocktail, a small risk that feels like a big step. He doesn't say a word about it, but I catch his grin while he scans the menu, and it makes me feel bold.

He orders nearly everything on the menu, and the food is just as incredible as he promised. Even when he dunks his sushi in peanut sauce—a move I find pretty unappealing—he just laughs at my expression and goads me into trying it. I refuse, of course, but it's a playful exchange that leaves us both smiling.

While he heads to the restroom, I flag down the waiter to cover the bill. I know the only way he'll let me pay is if he doesn't know I'm doing it. But the waiter returns with a sheepish grin, informing me that Jax had already left his credit card when he made the reservation.

I'm genuinely impressed. Whatever playbook he's working from, it's one every man should read.

On the ride home, my mind is a mess of conflicting emotions. I want Jax to come up, but I'm hesitant to ask. Not because I don't want him there—I do—but because I feel embarrassingly inexperienced when it comes to initiating anything more. I'm used to suppressing desire, not embracing it.

There's no parking out front, so I direct him to the underground garage. When he parks, he glances over at me.

"Can I walk you to your door?"

My heart races. "Would you... um, like to stay for a drink?" My cheeks flush as I stare at my hands.

Broken

"Are you sure? We don't have to—"

"I want you to," I blurt out, maybe a little too quickly. He smiles, gets out, and walks around to open my door. I take his hand, breathing through the nerves. We ride the elevator in silence, my eyes fixed on the floor, too shy to look at him.

At my door, I manage to unlock it without fumbling. Small victory.

Inside, I toss my jacket and bag onto the couch and kick off my shoes. I turn to him, not sure what comes next. It feels like standing at the edge of something huge, uncertain how to step forward.

I move closer, eyes still cast downward, until his scent surrounds me. He lifts my chin with one knuckle, guiding me to meet his gaze.

"What do you want to do, Ally?" he asks softly. When I don't answer he places one hand on my hip.

"Is this okay?"

I can't speak, but when I nod he brings my body flush against his.

"Do you want me to make you come?"

Broken

His voice is low and gravelly. My breath catches. "Yes."

He pulls me in closer, his hand still on my hip, and suddenly his lips crash against mine. He nudges us backward until the couch hits the backs of my knees, and I sink down, pulling him with me. He braces himself on one elbow, keeping his weight from crushing me, but his presence—his body pressing into mine—feels achingly good.

"God, I love kissing you. You taste incredible. I bet your cunt tastes even better."

The words are so filthy, so raw, that I freeze. A rush of heat and vulnerability collides inside me, overwhelming in its intensity. He must sense the shift because he pulls back slightly, eyes searching mine.

"I didn't mean to put any pressure on you. I was just thinking out loud," he murmurs gently.

I don't know how to respond, so I say nothing.

"Let's stick to the boundaries you've set. There's no need to rush," he adds.

I manage a quiet, grateful, "Okay."

Broken

His next kiss is softer, less urgent but just as consuming. There's a care in the way he touches me now, like he's tuning himself to my pace, not his.

His hand glides over my stomach and down between my thighs, still clothed in jeans.

"Is this okay?"

"Yes," I whisper.

He teases me through the fabric until I'm squirming, breath hitching with every stroke. A whimper escapes me when he pulls his hand away, but with a mischievous smirk, he reaches for the button of my jeans.

"Don't worry, beautiful. I'm not stopping."

He unfastens them with agonising slowness and slides them off, revealing my pink lace panties. His eyes darken.

"Pink is my new favourite colour," he murmurs.

His lips return to mine, then trail down my neck and along my collarbone. When his fingers slide over the lace, the friction sends sparks racing through me. He outlines the edge before slipping beneath it, fingers finding me wet and wanting.

Broken

"You're so wet for me," he whispers, lips grazing the curve of my breast where my shirt has ridden up.

I tug at the hem, and he helps me pull it over my head. With one hand, he unclasps my bra, and it joins the pile on the floor.

"Eyes on me, beautiful. Don't drift away."

His thumb circles my clit as his mouth finds my nipple, teasing and sucking through the lace before pulling it aside. One finger slides inside me—slow, deliberate, stretching me gently.

"I'm going to add another. Ready?"

I nod quickly, afraid he might stop.

He presses in, curling his fingers until my back arches off the couch. The pressure builds fast, a delicious ache just beneath the surface that's offset by the tight discomfort.

"More, please, Jax. I need more."

His movements quicken, his mouth still working my breast. I come apart beneath him, crying out as release rips through me in waves.

Broken

He doesn't stop, guiding me through it until I'm spent and trembling. Then, slowly, he pulls his fingers free and lifts them to his mouth.

"You're so sweet, I knew you would be" he breaths, savouring me like he's waited his whole life.

The sight undoes me, and I drag him down into a kiss—hungry and open—tasting myself on his tongue as it glides against mine, sending a wild rush through my body. With one hand gripping the back of his neck, pulling him closer, the other slides down to his jeans, finding him hard and ready beneath the denim. This time, I take control.

In a moment of boldness, I swiftly unfasten his jeans and slide them down over his hips, surprising myself with how assertive I feel. As I lower his boxers, his erection springs out, and the thrill of the moment fills me with confidence.

I grip him firmly, giving it a gentle stroke to see how he feels. He's rock solid and hot in my grasp, like a piece of steel covered in soft silk, and I can feel his warmth seeping into my hand. The hissing sound he makes boosts my confidence, encouraging me to keep going, again and again.

He's propped up on his elbow, one hand gripping my hip, his forehead resting against mine. His eyes are tightly shut, and he's breathing hard as I keep working him. I can't tear my gaze away; the look of pure pleasure on his face is like a drug, and it's thrilling to know I'm the one making him feel this way.

"Fuck, Ally. That feels incredible," he gasps out between breaths.

His hips begin to rock, and I pick up my rhythm to keep in sync with him. For a brief second, his body tenses right before it jerks, ropes of warm liquid spilling out of him to paint my stomach.

After a moment, his breathing steadies, and when he finally looks down at me, I can't help but beam with a huge smile.

He bends down and softly kisses me, his lips brushing against mine in a tender moment.

"Stay right there; I'll grab something to clean you up."

Broken

He sits up and steps away. As he walks off, my curiosity piques, and I can't help but swipe my finger through the mess on my stomach, bringing it to my lips. The taste is a mix of salty and just a hint of sweetness. I close my eyes, not just to enjoy the flavour but to fully immerse myself in the significance of what just happened.

I never imagined I'd find myself in a moment like this—there's no fear or anxiety, just a deep sense of intimacy.

This incredible man is fixing me, one touch at a time. When I finally open my eyes, I see him standing over me with that charming smirk that always makes my heart race. A wave of warmth floods my cheeks as I realise I'm blushing, completely caught off guard in this awkward yet thrilling moment.

"So, how does it taste?" he teases.

"It's sweeter than I thought it would be."

He laughs softly as he settles beside me, gently cleaning my stomach. The heat of the moment has faded, leaving me feeling a bit awkward and unsure about what to say or do next. Jax exudes this effortless confidence, while I can't shake the awareness of my almost bare state.

As I fumble to redress in my bra, he picks up my shirt from the floor and carefully slides it over my head and arms. I feel a mix of vulnerability and exposure, but there's something comforting about his presence. He stands up from the couch and takes my hand, helping me to my feet.

"It's getting late; I should get going," he says, and I can't help but feel a pang of disappointment. But then he cups my face in his hands and kisses me like time doesn't exist, and when he finally pulls away, I'm left breathless and floating.

He gets dressed in a hurry and slips out the door before I can even process what just happened.

Broken

CHAPTER 13

The next few days pass without anything particularly noteworthy. Jax is buried in work, so I haven't seen him, but he still sends messages throughout the day—which helps. To distract myself until Ty visits this weekend, I take on a couple of editing projects. I'm really hoping Ty comes alone this time. I'm already nervous enough about seeing my brother; I don't need Nate grilling me too.

Broken

It's 11AM on Saturday when I realise I haven't heard a word from Jax. Not even a good morning text. And somehow, that stings more than I expected. I was really looking forward to talking to him today, especially before Ty gets here. Now it just feels like I've missed my chance.

I send a quick message:

Ally: How's your day going?

Jax: Busy.

Ally: Do you have to work over the weekend?

Jax: If I did, you would be annoying me.

What. The. Fuck?

I stare at my phone, feeling thrown. Jax has never been short with me, let alone cold. I sit there, completely unsure of what to do next. Should I reply? Or should I give him space? I decide to go with something casual, something that won't make me seem needy—but still shows I'm not upset.

Ally: Have a nice weekend.

Twenty minutes pass with no response.

I realise I won't be getting one.

Broken

◆ ◆ ◆

It's a relief that Ty's distracted this weekend, caught up in his own romantic escapades and not paying much attention to me. Spending time with him is always easy —he's my favourite person for a reason.

Later that day, a text from Jax lights up my phone, and despite everything, my heart skips a beat.

Jax: Sorry about earlier. I had to work today and was dealing with a crisis over some coding issues.

Ally: No worries. We all have those days.

Jax: Have dinner with me?

Ally: I can't—my brother's visiting for the night.

Jax: What about tomorrow? Let me make it up to you for being rude.

Ally: I'd love to.

Jax: I'll pick you up at 6. Have a good night, beautiful x

◆ ◆ ◆

Broken

Just before 6 the next evening, I step out of the elevator and into the lobby. Jax walks through the entrance right on cue, spots me, and strides over. Without a word, he pulls me into his arms and kisses me like it's been far more than a few days.

"I missed you, beautiful," he whispers against my lips.

"I missed you too," I say, feeling the weight of those days apart more than I expected.

After another quick kiss, he grabs my hand and leads me to his car. The ride to dinner is comfortable and quiet. I shrug off my jacket and toss it in the backseat, resting my hand on his thigh. When I glance over at him, his smile does something wild to my heart.

"So... where are we going?" I ask.

"My local pub. It's chill, and the food's great."

I arch a brow, half-teasing. "You sure that's a good idea?"

He chuckles. "Trust me—I haven't embarrassed myself there like Ollie has."

Broken

I laugh, and as we drive through familiar streets, I joke that I should've driven, considering we're practically back at his place.

"Don't be ridiculous," he says. "I wanted to pick you up."

The parking lot is full, but we find a space at the far end. He's already opening my door by the time I unbuckle. When he takes my hand, I raise an eyebrow.

"And you say you're not a gentleman?"

"Chivalry isn't dead, beautiful." He winks, and damn it—my stomach does flips.

But as we walk toward the pub, that old, creeping sensation starts crawling up my spine. It's not rational —probably just a leftover twinge of paranoia—but it's there. Maybe it's the idea of meeting people from his world. Maybe it's the way he's starting to affect me physically in ways I didn't know I could still feel.

The pub has all the charm of a cozy English spot: padded booths, a big stone fireplace, warm lighting, and quirky little decorations on the shelves. Jax nods at a few people as we make our way to the bar— definitely a regular.

Broken

The bartender is young—probably younger than me—with a high ponytail and overly plumped lips, painted bright red. Her push-up bra is working overtime, and her high-waisted denim shorts might as well be underwear.

"Hey, Jax. The usual?" she purrs, blinking way too much mascara at him.

A wave of jealousy crashes over me before I can stop it. I'm not usually the jealous type, but something about her makes me want to claw her eyes out with a rusty spoon.

"Hey Carly. This is my girlfriend, Ally."

My heart stutters. *Girlfriend*?

Carly finally looks at me like I've just appeared out of thin air. I think she says something, but I don't hear it.

"She'll have a glass of Gembrook Hill," Jax says, pulling me back to reality.

I glance up at him, warmth spreading through my chest.

"I don't think we have that," Carly replies, all attitude.

Broken

"You do. I called ahead," he says smoothly, eyes still on me.

When she walks off, I lean in and whisper, "Girlfriend?"

He smirks—that smirk. "Aren't you?"

"Guess I am."

As he leads me out to the beer garden, I can't stop staring at him. His skinny jeans show off an ass I could bite, and that fitted grey tee clings to his biceps and tattoos in all the right ways.

He empties his pockets onto the table, then helps me climb over the bench seat. A few people say hello, and he introduces me as his girlfriend. My stomach flips every time I hear it.

"Wow, you sure are popular," I tease.

He shrugs. "This place is full of regulars. I stop by here a couple times a week when I'm working from home. Otherwise, I'd starve."

"I could live in isolation if it weren't for basic needs."

He laughs. "Same. But this place is easy. The food's good, and the people are decent."

Broken

I smirk. "Like the bartender?"

As soon as it's out, I regret it.

"Are you jealous, Ally?"

Asshole.

"What? No, definitely not."

"I haven't been with her. I wouldn't bring you here if I had." He leans in and kisses me, completely unfazed by the crowd.

Over dinner, I polish off my second glass of wine. Jax sticks to two beers since he's driving. I suggest we Uber, but he looks almost hurt, so I drop it.

"You good if I run to the bathroom?"

"Of course."

"I'll grab my second beer on the way back. Want another wine?"

"No, I'm good—actually, yeah. One more."

It's been forever since I've had more than one drink in public—only ever with Tyler—but with Jax, I feel safe. The wind picks up, and I shiver, remembering my jacket is still in the car. I spot his keys on the table and figure I can grab it quickly.

Broken

The parking lot is well-lit, and I'm not far. For once, I'm not afraid. Jax has changed something in me—given me confidence I didn't think I'd feel again. I want to fit into his life. I want to see where this goes. With him, fear doesn't hold the same power.

I reach the car and press the unlock button, leaning into the back seat for my jacket.

But as I'm stepping back, someone slams into me, forcing me against the side of the car. A hand wraps tight around my throat.

CHAPTER 14

*T*his isn't real. *This isn't real. This isn't real.* The mantra echoes relentlessly in my mind, but the truth is inescapable. This *is* real. This *is* happening. Again.

"I missed you, Banana."

That name. That voice. Those piercing blue eyes. His words scrape against my skin like sandpaper—abrasive, unbearable. I want to scream, but I doubt I could even if his hand wasn't clamped around my throat. Fear has me paralysed, locking my body in a vice grip. In an instant, I'm 16 again—unable to move, unable to breathe, unable to think.

My deepest fears are staring me down. It's like the embodiment of my nightmares has come to life.

Michael...

"I'm going to let go, and you're not going to scream. Do you understand?"

I nod, hard and fast, gasping as he finally releases my throat. Air floods my lungs like a lifeline—but just as I suck in a breath to scream, his hand slams back against my neck, silencing me.

The sickening crack of his slap rings in my ears. His weight crushes me, his arousal pressed firmly against my thigh.

"Four years and you still want to scream like a bitch. Some people never learn."

The bitter irony of his words isn't lost on me.

"How?" I croak, my voice barely a whisper, raw with disbelief and fear.

"My dad believed I'd finally learned from my mistakes," he says with a dark chuckle. "I convinced him I was on the right path. But Mum and Nat weren't buying it. I told him I'd leave the past behind and show them I could contribute to society. By Christmas, they'd come around."

His gaze is wild, frenzied, like he's looking straight through me.

I've never liked the nickname Banana—but I never hated it either. It didn't bother me much—until I started to associate it with Michael and the beach. Now it's tainted, a trigger, dragging me back into the very memory playing out in real time. I feel powerless. Frozen.

"I haven't stopped thinking about you, Banana. Finding you wasn't hard; I just had to wait it out. I knew Tyler and Nate would eventually lead me to you."

It hits me like a punch— Nate was here two weeks ago.

He's been watching me all this time.

He leans in, his tongue brushing my cheek, licking away tears I hadn't even realised were falling. I flinch, stomach churning.

Broken

"You can only imagine how stunned I was when I followed you to that guy's place last week. And again tonight."

Panic crashes through me. He knows about Jax.

Fuck. He knows about Jax.

He's going to hurt him.

"So tell me, have you spread your legs for him? Let him touch what's *mine*? I can't stand the thought of someone else touching you. I had it all planned out, but when I saw you out here alone, I had to act. You're meant to be with me."

His free hand finds its way between my thighs. I can feel his breath against my ear, sending shivers of revulsion down my spine. My mind spirals, the air turns thin, and I wish I could just disappear, just float away from this nightmare.

"I've thought about you every single day. How good you felt around me. How tight you were. Feel what you do to me?"

He presses himself harder against my leg. Another wave of nausea rolls over me.

Broken

"I've waited four fucking long years to feel you again. Trust me—you're going to love this. Just like you did the first time."

His fingers fumble with the button on my jeans, sliding down the zip. Each metallic click screams in my ears.

His tongue flicks across my cheek again, collecting more tears, as his hand slips into my jeans.

"GET THE FUCK OFF HER!"

That voice. I know that voice.

In a sudden blur, Michael's weight vanishes. It happens so fast, it feels like it was never real to begin with. I hit the ground hard, curling up into a tight ball, arms clutching around my knees. I bury myself in my body, desperate to disappear. My mind is chaos. I can't stop shaking.

Where's Jax? I just want Jax.

Every sound around me is too loud—grunts, thuds, voices—but I can't make sense of any of it. Then, a gentle hand brushes the back of my head. A waft of sweet floral perfume reaches me.

Female. Not a threat.

Broken

She sits beside me, pulling me close. I lean into her warmth instinctively, like it's the only thing keeping me from falling apart.

A loud crack splits the air, making me flinch violently, but still, I can't open my eyes. The shouting blurs into background noise. Then a large, rough hand lands on my knee—

Male. *Threat.*

I jerk away and scream.

"Shh, you're okay. I've got you," a high-pitched voice murmurs in my ear, gentle, soothing. She rocks me, running her fingers through my hair. "The police are on their way. Can I call someone for you?"

"I just want Jax."

My voice is ragged, each word painful, but I force them out.

"Ally?"

His voice slices through the fog in my brain, clear and real. I crack open my eyes.

He's there. Right in front of me, crouched down, his gorgeous face twisted in worry. His hands are up, palms facing me, as if to say *I'm safe. It's just me.*

Broken

I lunge at him, so fast and so hard that he falls back onto the ground with me in his arms. He holds me tight, one hand tangled in my hair, stroking too quickly to be soothing, the other gripping me close.

At that moment, nothing else exists. I melt into him, into his scent, into the only place that feels like safety.

CHAPTER 15

I'm in shock. I've been here before, and it's no more inviting than the first time I visited this realm. I wasn't present when the cops tried to talk to me, nor did I see the paramedics checking me over. I have no clue about my injuries, but they can't be too serious since I'm in Jax's car. I vaguely recall making a scene when someone brought up the hospital —I must've been insistent enough to get my way, demanding the safe zone of my apartment. The only moment I truly tuned in was when I heard Michael's

Broken

name. Instantly, my fight-or-flight response kicked in, and I became hyper-aware. Apparently, he's got a broken jaw and was taken away in an ambulance under police guard.

Suddenly, I blink and find myself at my front door, like I've been watching from outside my own body. Jax fumbles with a bunch of keys, trying to find the right one. I take them from him on autopilot and slide one into the lock. The door swings open, and I head straight down the hallway with a fierce need to scrub myself clean. The urge to wash my skin off my bones is so strong that I start stripping before I'm even vaguely aware the door's being pulled shut behind me.

Once I'm under the water, everything hits me. Hard. I break down. Tears pour down my face. My body trembles, legs like jelly. My arm stings from scrubbing so hard, but the filthy feeling won't go away. I sink to the floor, curling up against the wall with my knees tight to my chest, letting the water wash over me as I try to drown out my memories.

◆ ◆ ◆

Broken

A faint knocking breaks through the roar of the water, followed by his voice.

"Ally, are you okay, beautiful?"

I snapped back to reality a while ago, but my voice seems to have vanished.

"You've been in there nearly an hour. I'm starting to get worried."

Still, I don't respond.

"If you don't answer me, I'm coming in."

The door creaks open, but I can't muster the strength to lift my forehead from my knees. The water shifts direction, then stops. I raise my head just enough to see Jax standing outside the shower, holding a towel across the door. His head is tipped up, eyes fixed on the ceiling, giving me privacy.

With a deep breath, I force myself to stand and take a step towards him. He quickly wraps the towel around me, careful to avoid any sore spots, and grabs another from the shelf. He squeezes the water from my hair a few times before drying my arms, then crouches down to gently pat my legs dry. Once he's done, he takes my hand and leads me to the bedroom, sitting me on the edge of the bed. I catch a glimpse of him pulling off his T-shirt, and before I know it, he's easing it over my head, guiding my arms into the sleeves. The fabric envelopes me, warm and soft, carrying his scent like a protective shield. I instantly feel safe.

"I'm sorry," I whisper.

He freezes and I feel him look down at me, but I keep my gaze on the floor.

"You've got nothing to be sorry for—"

"I'm sorry I didn't tell you all of it."

He sighs heavily and squats down to my eye level.

"Ally, when you were sixteen, did he…"

He can't finish, but I know what he's asking.

"Yes."

"Was that your first time?"

"Yes."

He mutters a curse under his breath.

"Have you ever been touched consensually?"

"Yes. There was this one guy," I reply, trying to lighten the mood. He gives a strained smile, realising I'm talking about him.

Broken

"Why isn't he behind bars?"

"I made a deal. I agreed not to file charges in exchange for a settlement and his commitment to stay in a psychiatric facility full-time."

"Why the fuck would you do that?" He replies, anger dripping from his voice.

"To protect Tyler." I shrug like it's the most obvious thing in the world. Tyler had just turned 18—technically an adult—but his whole future was still ahead of him. I couldn't ruin that just because he stepped in to protect me.

When I finally meet Jax's eyes, there's no pity, no anger, not even empathy. Just calm, like he's trying to absorb the weight of my reality.

"Ty lost Natalie that night. She was everything to him, and their families tore them apart. I wasn't going to ruin his future too."

The silence stretches between us.

"If you want to leave, I totally understand. You should be running for the door right about now."

"Why would I run?"

Broken

He tucks my damp hair behind my ear and kisses my forehead.

"Just tell me what you need."

"Will you stay with me tonight?"

"I'm not going anywhere."

"Can you help me forget?"

He hesitates. "Are you really ready for that?"

I know it doesn't make sense—to want this now—but I need to reclaim this moment. I need to feel something that doesn't hurt.

"Yes."

He kisses me, tentative at first, like he's checking for hesitation. There is none. My hands find his neck, pulling him closer as the kiss deepens. Our tongues dance, breaths mingling. I explore his chest, fingers tracing every line of muscle, grounding myself in him.

I take his hands and place them on my thighs, silently asking for more.

"Lie back and keep your eyes on me," he murmurs.

He shifts beside me, propped on one elbow, his fingers drawing slow, soft circles on my thigh.

"If you want to stop, just say so."

Broken

"Stop treating me like I'm made of glass."

His eyes search mine, then something in him breaks. His lips crash onto mine, his hand sliding up beneath his shirt on me, lifting the fabric to reveal bare skin.

His fingers close around my nipple, teasing, and I arch into his touch. He breaks the kiss only to trail his lips down my neck, over my collarbone, and to my breast, tongue circling, lips sucking gently. I gasp, my body vibrating with sensation.

He's everywhere—his weight grounding me, his scent surrounding me, his hands and mouth claiming every part of me. I run my fingers through his hair, tugging lightly, and he groans. Our eyes lock. Desire burns bright in his.

He bites gently, teasing my other nipple. The tension coils inside me, sharp and sweet. Waves of pleasure ripple through me—unexpected, intense, overwhelming.

Embarrassed, I start to cover my face, but he gently pulls my hand away.

"I love how your body responds to me."

Broken

His voice is intoxicating—rough and soft all at once. I groan, cheeks flushing.

"Feeling any better, beautiful?" he teases.

"Not yet," I reply, shifting my position to straddle him, one leg draped over his lap. I push gently on his shoulders, guiding him down, and lean in to kiss him.

His fingers weave through my hair while the other hand finds its way to cup the side of my neck, and I can't help but wince at the pressure; I haven't dared to check for any marks yet, but I can only imagine the evidence of the earlier assault. Instantly, he pulls his hand away, trying to break the kiss, but I can't resist the urge to grind against him, feeling the hard outline of his erection through his jeans.

The friction sends a wave of heat through me, and I can sense the wetness pooling on my thighs as I pick up the pace, unsure if I'm even doing it right, but his heavy breathing and low groans tell me he's definitely enjoying it. I pull away from his lips, trailing kisses down his neck and across his chest, following the dark line of hair that leads to his waistband.

Broken

Just as I reach for his button, his hand catches my wrist, halting my movements. His voice is soft and reassuring when he says, "You don't have to."

I can't help but let my gaze wander over his body, taking in the sight of him propped up on one elbow, his gentle eyes fixed on me.

"I want to." I need this. I've never craved anything more than to taste him right now. I need to regain control of my body and what I do with it. That thought is empowering.

"Have you done this before?" he asks, his concern evident as he wonders if this might trigger any memories for me. I can't help but smile at his thoughtfulness as I reply,

"No. This is new."

As he releases my wrist, I eagerly dive into getting his pants off, my excitement pushing me to act quickly. I know I should probably take a moment to think it through, but that thought barely registers as I deftly undo his button and slide down the zipper. I tug at the sides of his jeans while he lifts his hips, silently cursing the snug fit. I manage to free one leg before

Broken

I'm back kneeling between his legs, determined. With a swift motion, I push his boxers down, and his cock springs free, resting on his stomach—long, smooth, and hard, with a neatly trimmed patch of hair.

Still propped up on one elbow, he tips my chin, urging me to meet his gaze.

"You don't have to…" But I brush his hand away and take the tip of his cock into my mouth. He falls back onto the bed, groaning, as he gathers my hair into a messy pile on top of my head, keeping it out of my face. Even when he's getting his dick sucked, this man is considerate.

I swirl my tongue around the head, tasting the salty bead of moisture that forms at the slit. When I try to slide my lips down his length, I encounter some friction, forcing me to release him just long enough to wet my lips and try again.

My lips glide down his shaft and back up repeatedly, taking him as deep as I can before gagging. I pull back and suck hard on the crown of his cock and his stomach clenched. My hand wraps around his base and moves in time with my mouth, sliding up and down his cock.

I feel him get even harder in my mouth—if that's even possible—and I can see the muscles in his stomach tightening up. His breathing is heavy, and his fingers are digging into my scalp, sending shivers down my spine. When he finally speaks, his voice is rough.

"Ally, it's been a while. I'm not going to last much longer."

He takes a sharp breath and adds, "You need to stop if you don't want me to come... in your mouth."

But honestly, that just makes me want to go faster. My hand and lips working him with urgency, eager to wash away that imaginary taste of bile from earlier.

I can feel his entire body tense up, jerk and then go completely still just before warm, salty fluid floods my mouth. I keep going, not quite sure when to pull back, until he finally relaxes, and I swallow it down. With a soft pop, I pull him out of my mouth, and he's instantly on me, tucking my hair behind my ears, and kissing me deeply. He must taste himself on my tongue, but it doesn't seem to bother him at all as our tongues intertwine.

"That was fucking incredible."

I can feel my cheeks heat up from the compliment.

"Now it's my turn."

In a flash, Jax flips me onto my back and lowers his head between my legs. He plants a teasing kiss on my pubic bone, glancing up at me to check if it's okay to continue.

I can barely manage a nod, my voice completely lost in the moment. The first stroke of his tongue sends me spiralling into bliss, and I feel like I'm seeing stars. He skilfully licks from my clit down to my entrance and back up again, circling my sensitive spot and repeating the delicious motion. The roughness of his stubble against my inner thighs contrasts beautifully with the soft, tantalising movements of his tongue. As he gently probes my entrance with his finger, his lips wrap around my clit, sucking with determination.

He slides one finger inside me, moving it in a circular motion to stretch me, then adds a second finger and a third. The sensation is a mix of discomfort and pleasure, but with his lips working their magic on my clit, it's manageable.

He pumps his fingers deeper, curling them just right to hit that secret spot I recently found out existed, and suddenly, I'm completely undone.

His fingers still, but his lips keep their rhythm, guiding me through the most intense experience I've ever had.

After a long, exhausting night, my body finally relaxes, a light sheen of sweat covering my skin. As I open my eyes, I see him lying beside me, propped up on his side, intently studying my face. A rush of warmth spreads through me from his gaze, and I instinctively turn to bury my face against his chest, seeking refuge.

He shifts, pulling me up with him until we're tucked under the blankets. He wraps his arm around me, holding me close.

"Get some sleep, beautiful. It's been a long day."

I hum softly, already drifting off. As I melt into him, one thought echoes through my mind: *Today would've broken me—if he hadn't been here.*

Broken

CHAPTER 16

I woke up to an empty bed, and a wave of ice-cold dread washed over me. Sunlight streamed in through the gap in the curtains, painting stripes across the space where Jax had slept.

Memories from last night flooded back in a chaotic rush: the pub, the parking lot, Michael, the attack, the shower, the intense orgasm…

My heart hammered against my ribs. Had he left? Had I finally scared him off?

Broken

Last night, I'd finally opened up about... everything. All the messy, ugly parts of my past that I usually kept locked away. I'd been so vulnerable, letting him see the broken pieces I tried so hard to hide.

And now, the silence screamed that I'd made a mistake.

Maybe I was too much. Maybe Jax, like everyone else, couldn't handle the truth about me.

I pulled the covers tighter, the fabric doing little to ward off the chill that settles deep in my bones. I lay there, paralysed by the fear of facing the truth—of him being gone.

"Because, dickhead, it may be Monday, but I called in sick. I'm at my girlfriend's house. I'm working off a fucking phone here. We don't all carry around a fucking laptop everywhere we go."

He's in the kitchen. The angry whispering is unmistakable—low, irritable, and very much Jax.

Relief washes over me.

I grab a pair of underwear from the drawer beside the bed and follow the sound of his voice.

Broken

There he is, leaning against the counter, jeans on but shirtless, hair tousled in that just-woke-up way that makes him look edible. I glance down and smile—I'm still wearing his shirt.

"You can use my laptop if that helps," I offer, voice soft and raspy as I gingerly touch the tender spots on my neck.

He looks up, startled, but quickly abandons his phone and rushes over, cradling my face in his hands.

I melt into his touch, the gratitude overwhelming as he presses a gentle kiss to my lips.

"Did I wake you?" he asks, the irritation in his voice replaced by warmth.

"No, I was already awake," I reply, tension easing.

"I'm sorry you woke up alone."

"Don't be. Everything okay?"

"Yeah, just a work emergency."

"Use my laptop if it'll help."

"It'll only take a few minutes."

He steals another kiss before heading back to the counter and grabbing his phone.

"Yeah, yeah, I'm still here, asshole," he mutters.

Broken

Then, with a snort, "You're just jealous I don't talk to you like that."

I move towards the coffee machine, trying not to make any noise while Jax sets his phone on speaker and gets to work.

When I glance back, I can't help but stare—his fingers dance over the keyboard, eyes glued to a screen that looks straight out of The Matrix. I consider myself decent with tech, but this? This is some next-level shit.

Watching him in his element? Is fucking hot.

I've never cared much about what he does for work, but maybe I should start paying attention.

As if he senses my gaze, he shoots me a smirk without missing a beat on the keys.

"If you have any other issues, well… don't fucking call me. Bye."

He hangs up, shuts the laptop, and strolls over, nudging me gently until my back hits the counter. His hands slide up my spine.

"What's that look for, huh?" he teases.

"You're kind of hot." I laugh softly, and he grins.

"Aren't all firemen?"

Broken

I roll my eyes and bury my head against his chest, earning a laugh from him.

And then I hear the front door click open.

Fuck.

Jax steps back as I look up—Tyler's in the doorway.

This is *not* going to go well.

He looks furious, and honestly, I can't blame him. I'm pants-less. Jax is shirtless. Tyler looks like someone just kicked his puppy.

Nate's behind him, frozen in place, face caught between confusion and awkward amusement. Tyler, on the other hand, radiates serial-killer energy.

"What are you doing here?" I demand.

Nate, always the diplomat, squeezes Ty's shoulder as he sidesteps him.

"Good morning to you too, Banana. Your phone's off," he chirps.

"Don't call me that," I snap automatically.

I move away from Jax, trying to put distance between him and me.

Broken

Nate approaches, plants a kiss on my hair, and tilts my chin up. He sees the bruising on my neck, and his face tightens.

"How're you feeling this bright and sunny morning?"

"I'm fine. Why are you here?"

"Nat called."

"Shit," I mutter.

"Who's the eye candy?" Nate asks, nodding toward Jax.

A low growl comes from the doorway—Tyler, still glaring at Jax like he's imagining twenty different ways to kill him.

I'm officially over this.

"The eye candy is the reason Michael will be eating through a straw for the next six to eight weeks," I shoot back.

"So you brought him home?" Nate sounds unimpressed.

"He's my boyfriend."

Jax stands tall, calm in the face of all this tension.

Broken

"Jesus, Banana! I'm too pretty to go to jail," Nate says dramatically.

"Don't call me that!"

To my surprise, he turns to Jax and extends a hand.

"I'm Nate. The friendly one over there is Tyler." he says, nodding towards the doorway

Jax shakes his hand, and the room lightens just a fraction.

"How does Nat know?" I ask, still suspicious. It isn't the most pressing issue at the moment but I need to know how my brother has a direct line of information into my life.

"The hospital had to contact next of kin," Nate replies, eyes still assessing Jax.

Of course they did.

"So, boyfriend… how do you know Banana?"

And just like that, I snap.

"DON'T CALL ME THAT!"

The shout rips out of me, straining my throat. I wince and instinctively touch my neck.

Jax starts to take a step closer, but Nate quickly put a hand out to stop him. Out of the corner of my eye, I catch Tyler crossing the room and wraps me in a hug that nearly knocks the breath out of me.

He kisses the top of my head, then holds me at arm's length, scanning me.

"Seriously, Ty, I'm fine."

His gaze lingers on my bruised neck and I can see the tension in his jaw..

"Were you looked over?"

I hesitate. I remember being in an ambulance at some point, but after that, everything's a blur.

"Just some bruising and shock, nothing serious," Jax chimes in, trying to be helpful, but Tyler doesn't look away from me.

"Hannah?"

Well. Fuck.

I glance at Jax, panic clawing its way up my chest. But he's calm. So fucking calm. He's exuding a sense of control that makes me feel a little more at ease. Tyler steps into my view, crouches slightly, so we're at eye level, his gaze probing me with unspoken questions.

Broken

"No. I promise. Jax stopped him," I whisper, just for him.

He exhales, running a hand through his hair.

"Good. That's good. Get dressed—we're going out for breakfast," he says firmly, leaving no room for argument, but a wave of panic grips me like a jolt of electricity.

"What? No. I'm not going."

I know what he's doing. And I should be grateful. But all I can think about is the last time this happened.

After the first incident, I'd locked myself away for five months. I was a hermit—afraid, ashamed, and constantly on edge. Crying whenever someone got too close to me. It was Tyler and, to some extent, Nate who picked up the pieces, acting as my safety net and coaxing me back into the world, but that also made me reliant on them. It took nearly a year before I could step outside without Tyler by my side.

Moving here alone had been monumental—a declaration of independence.

Now, it feels like he's throwing me back into the deep end to prevent me from slipping backward.

Broken

"Ally, get dressed. You can bring your *boyfriend*, but we're going out. End of story."

I glance at Nate, hoping for an ally. He just gives me a knowing smile.

Well. Fuck.

I guess I'm going out.

CHAPTER 17

I throw on my clothes in a hurry, anxious about leaving Jax alone with my brother and his buddy for too long. I don't even check what I'm wearing, but I make sure to slip on my silver glitter light-up Sketchers—my 'I don't take shit' shoes. I actually feel okay, anxiety still sleeping off the adrenaline of the last twenty-four hours—until I step out of the elevator and see the outside world.

Instinctively, I grab Jax's hand like it's a lifeline, squeezing it a little too hard. He glances down at our hands for a moment but just squeezes back, and the simple gesture is more reassuring than anything he could say.

We walk the two blocks, me tucked between Jax and Ty, until we reach the coffee shop Tyler and I usually hit up on Sunday mornings. Normally, there's a five-minute wait for a table, and true to routine, Ty—despite his tough-love style—heads straight for a quiet corner inside instead of making us wait outside. He knows being out in the open will trigger a panic attack, and I appreciate that small kindness more than I can say.

Once we finally sit down, it hits me how awkward this is going to be. I'm grateful Jax is here, but this is prime territory for disaster. Thankfully, Nate jumps in before Tyler's patented 'go screw yourself' vibe gets out of hand.

"So, *boyfriend*, what do you do?" he asks.

"Jax. His name is Jax," I say, irritation already creeping in.

Jax chuckles at my tone. "I work in IT."

Ty snorts. "No, you don't."

Broken

Jax just shrugs. "Yeah, I really do."

Ty rolls his eyes. "Come on, you're way too easy on the eyes to be a nerd. You look like you should be rescuing kittens from trees."

I choke on my water and end up sputtering it all over the table, caught mid-sip in a fit of coughing. Jax is practically in stitches, slapping my back while trying to catch his breath. Jerk.

"Jesus, Ally, were you raised in a barn or something?" Nate laughs as I frantically dab at the mess with a napkin.

"Nope. Just around you wild animals," I shoot back.

"Oh, come on! You were the worst one of us. Did you tell your boyfriend about the time you laughed so hard at the school fair that you ended up peeing yourself?"

My cheeks flush. "I was seven, Nate."

"What about the time you ignored the instructions on that fake tan in a can and looked like an Oompa Loompa for three days?" Tyler adds, barely breathing between laughs.

Broken

"And let's not forget those jeans you insisted on wearing even though they didn't fit anymore—'cause they were super cute—and they split right up the back in the middle of the shopping centre!"

They're howling like kids. Even Jax is struggling to keep a straight face.

"Remember when you got your period—"

"Okay, that's enough!" I cut Nate off, pointing at him first. "Your sister caught you playing dress-up in her clothes more than once," I snap, then turn to Tyler. "And you were caught jacking off by your own mother."

Jax completely loses it, laughing harder than ever.

"Yeah, but we don't get embarrassed and turn into a tomato like you do," Tyler teases.

Someone bumps into the back of my chair, and I instantly tense. I'd been so caught up in the mortification that I forgot about my anxiety. It hits me all at once, sharper than before.

Thankfully, Jax's hand finds its way to my thigh, giving it a reassuring squeeze. I let out a slow breath and start to relax again.

Broken

The rest of breakfast goes by without any more embarrassing stories, and the guys manage to keep it mostly civil. They're not exactly getting along, but Ty doesn't look like he wants to skin Jax alive anymore.

To everyone's horror, Jax orders peanut butter on toast topped with scrambled eggs. The collective gag around the table somehow lightens the mood.

After two glasses of water and a strong coffee, I realise I really need to pee, but the idea of walking across the room alone makes my stomach turn. My leg starts bouncing beneath the table, but Tyler launches into a long story about some vintage car he and Nate are restoring, which means we're not moving any time soon.

I catch Nate's eye and give him my best pleading look. I'm already out of my seat when he stands and casually says he's heading to the bathroom.

Still, I can't shake the feeling that leaving Tyler and Jax alone is a very bad idea.

"Stop being dramatic. I'm not going to bite him," Tyler mutters, like he read my mind.

Broken

"Thank you," I whisper to Nate as he walks me across the room.

"Don't thank me," he says, side-eying the table. "Your brother's gonna chew my ass, and your boyfriend's definitely going to start wondering if there's something going on here."

I glance back. Sure enough, Jax is watching with a furrowed brow.

❖ ❖ ❖

The walk home feels easier somehow. I still cling to Jax until we're safely back inside my building, but I owe Ty a lot for dragging me out instead of letting me spiral.

Once we reach the lobby, Jax turns to me. "I'm going to head home, let you spend some time with your brother."

I try not to let the disappointment show, but Tyler surprises me.

"Stick around, boyfriend. We're having fun," he says, tone almost friendly, but with an edge that makes me nervous.

Broken

"Oh no, I'm sure he has to go," I say quickly, shooting Jax a silent please.

But Jax just grins. "I can stay."

Shit.

We barely get through the door before Tyler snatches up my keys and grabs a couple of beers from the fridge.

"Ally, I haven't checked your car in a while. I'm gonna give it a once-over. You know anything about cars, boyfriend?"

Oh no. This is it. Classic big brother interrogation.

"Not really. I can change a tire. Basics," Jax replies calmly, way more chill than I feel.

Tyler throws an arm around Jax's shoulders. "Come on, then. Let's teach you a thing or two."

I glance at Nate, who's standing now, visibly tense.

"I'm always up to learn something new," Nate says, clearly trying to tag along.

Tyler waves him off. "You're a qualified mechanic, dickhead. What are you going to learn? Sit down and fire up the PlayStation. We won't be long."

Fuck my life.

Broken

I last ten minutes before the urge to rescue Jax becomes too strong. I grab a couple of beers from the fridge and tell Nate I'm taking them out, then bolt for the elevator.

My hands are slick with sweat despite the cold bottles, and my heart's racing like mad. Our parking spot isn't far, just tucked behind a concrete pillar near the lift.

When the doors open, I don't hear yelling, just voices—so I hover just inside the elevator to eavesdrop.

"About six weeks. We met at a bar in the city," Jax says, his tone calm.

"She doesn't go to bars," Tyler snaps.

"She was there with your girlfriend. Ash."

Christ. Don't poke the bear.

"Great. So this is *my* fault. And her name wasn't Ash, it was... something like Kylie or whatever."

Jax laughs. "No, it wasn't."

Tyler mutters, "She was a total bimbo, but great tits."

Jax responds smoothly, "Really? I didn't notice."

Broken

Liar. He definitely noticed. It was hard not to, but the fact that he isn't acknowledging it puts a stupid smile on my face. Ty is testing him and he's passing with flying colours.

There's a pause. Then Tyler's tone shifts.

"Is she still having nightmares?"

"She hasn't mentioned it, but I can't say for sure."

"She wakes up screaming," Tyler says flatly.

"I wouldn't know," Jax replies.

The silence after that is heavy. I peek around the corner. Tyler is bent over the hood of my car, but he's not looking at the engine. His eyes are on Jax, who's leaning against a pillar, looking steady as ever.

The elevator dings again, and someone steps out. My panic spikes and I slip back inside, heading straight up to the apartment.

Nate glances at me as I walk in, raising a brow at the beers.

"Oh, uh, they weren't killing each other, so I figured I'd let them be."

He gives me a puzzled look, but turns back to the TV.

Broken

When the guys return, it's not tense, but it's not exactly cheerful either. Still, no one looks murdered. That's a win.

Jax says goodbye, and to my total shock, Tyler actually shakes his hand. This is not how I imagined today would go. Jax leans down to kiss my forehead and says he'll call me later.

I stare at the closed door until Tyler clears his throat.

"Seriously, wipe that shit-eating grin off your face. It's creeping me out."

I hadn't even realised I was smiling.

"So?" I ask, hesitant. "What do you think?"

"He seems okay."

My jaw practically hits the floor. Nate stares at Tyler like he's just grown a second head.

Ty just shrugs. "What? You could do worse."

"Oh my god. You actually like him!" My voice squeaks with disbelief.

"No, I don't."

"Yes, you do!" I'm grinning so hard it hurts. Never in my wildest dreams did I think I'd have a boyfriend, let alone one that my brother would approve of.

Broken

"What the fuck did he say?" Nate asks, sounding just as baffled as I feel.

"Nothing."

"Come on—he must've said *something* for you to decide not to kill him."

I'm desperate to uncover the secret so I can share it with anyone else who might meet my brother in the future.

Tyler stays quiet.

"Tell me what made you like him!" I urge through my laughter.

"Fine, he said he doesn't know if you have nightmares," Tyler replies, still glued to his game.

"What?…" Nate chuckles, and then it hits me like a ton of bricks.

"You like him because I'm not sleeping with him."

Tyler shrugs. "Well, yeah. Poor guy's balls are probably gonna fall off from being so blue. If he were dating a normal person, I'd think he was—shit. I didn't mean that."

My smile and laughter vanish instantly, crushed by the freight train of my brother's words. All the insecurities and fears I've battled over the past three years come crashing down on me. If the person I'm closest to doesn't think I'm normal, what chance do I have at a normal relationship?

Nate looks at me like I'm about to explode, and Tyler's face is filled with regret, but I feel completely numb. A meltdown is looming, but for now, I'm just blank.

"Ally, I'm sorry. I—"

"No, it's fine. I get it," My voice is flat. "Someone like me could never be normal, right? Could never not be broken."

"Ally—"

"I mean, how could I *not* be seen as damaged? I'm just a product of what Michael made me. It's ridiculous to think I could have a normal relationship. Selfish, even. Why pretend, when he could be with someone who doesn't come with all my fucked-up issues? And let's be real—how gay must he be to be okay with not fucking me, right? That's what you're both thinking?"

"Fuck *no*!" Nate snaps. "This idiot doesn't get to speak for me."

Broken

But it's too late. The hurt is already there.

"Could you lock the door on your way out?" I say quietly. "Excuse me."

I kick off my shoes. My 'I don't take shit' shoes feel like a joke now. I walk straight to the bathroom, lock the door, and stare at myself in the mirror.

Bruises linger around my neck. A reminder.

I'm not just hurting on the outside. I'm bruised all the way through.

Broken

CHAPTER 18

I spent over two hours in that bathroom, listening to their desperate attempts to reach me. Eventually, they realised they were fighting a losing battle and decided to leave. It was a barrage of apologies and threats, with one particularly low moment when Ty said, "Jax messaged you. Don't you want to know what it says?"

The tears I'd been quietly shedding had dried up after the first hour, but I still couldn't bring myself to face them. I just wanted to drown in my own sorrow, away from prying eyes. I do appreciate that they took the day off work to check on me—especially since Ty was just here yesterday—but honestly, I'm not in the best shape, and I'd rather they didn't have to see me like this.

Eventually, I managed to peel myself off the cold bathroom floor and stumbled to my emergency stash, taking a hefty swig of tequila before grabbing my phone to check the message.

Jax: Sorry I'm late; had to rescue a kitten from
a tree. Where do you see yourself in five
years?

I read it over and over. After the third time, I locked the screen and set the phone down. I realised I can't keep doing this—with him, to him. So I leave my phone on the counter and take the tequila bottle to bed.

◆ ◆ ◆

There's an excessive buzzing in my head. I don't remember when I drifted off, but when I wake, it's dark outside and I'm still drunk from the half bottle of tequila. The buzzing had subsided for a moment, but as soon as I close my eyes to stave off the dizziness, it comes roaring back.

What the fuck?

It takes my tequila-soaked brain way too long to realise the noise is coming from the next room. I clumsily get out of bed, tripping over my own feet as I make my way to the front door. I fling it open, but there's nobody there. Strange—I could have sworn I heard something. Just as I'm about to think more on it, the buzzing cuts through my thoughts again.

I hit the intercom button and, in a voice far too flirty for my own good, I say, "Well, hello there." Clearly, too much tequila has turned me into a hooker looking for a good time.

"I apologise for the interruption, Miss Barlowe, but there's a gentleman here requesting a wellness check."

"A gentleman? Sounds intriguing! What's he like? Does he have honey-coloured eyes and abs just begging to be licked?"

Broken

The voice on the other end clears his throat, sounding a bit uncomfortable. "His eyes are golden brown, but I can't really comment on the lickable abs—I'm sorry."

"Jesus Christ, Ally, are you drunk?" His smooth, familiar voice seems to come from far away, like he's in another room.

"Hey, Jax, did you get to slide down any poles today?" I ask, bursting into giggles.

Another throat clear before the first voice asks, "Shall I send him and his lickable abs up to you?"

"God, yes! But only if he takes his shirt off first."

I dash to the bathroom, quickly brushing my teeth—I'm not that drunk to forget I must taste like straight tequila. A knock interrupts me, and I glide across the living room to answer it, only to be hit with a wave of disappointment when I see Jax is still wearing a T-shirt. I slam the door in his bewildered face, then swing it open again—nope, still not shirtless.

The moment he steps inside, I'm all over him—my fingers in his hair, my body pressed against his, my lips desperate to find their mark. He holds me at arm's length, a teasing grin on his face.

"How drunk are you?" he asks, clearly amused.

"Drunk enough to want you," I reply, pushing against his grip and moulding myself against him. My fingers dig into his warm, hard muscles as I scratch at his chest. He doesn't push me away, but my lips barely graze his neck before he grips my shoulders and pulls me back again.

"I was worried about you. I must have called and texted you a dozen times," he says.

"Sorry, I was busy hanging out with my friend tequila," I shoot back.

"Well, she sounds like a blast," he says with a wry grin.

"Shut up and fuck me," I demand.

His body tenses, but I'm too far gone to notice the shift in mood.

"What's gotten into you?" he asks, puzzled.

"What's the matter, Jax? Don't you want to fuck me?" I tease, trying to keep it light.

Broken

"Of course I do—it's all I think about. But not like this. Not when you're drunk," he says gently.

His rejection hits me harder than expected. I throw my hands up, defensive.

"Seriously? Ty's right! Maybe you are gay!"

His eyebrows shoot up in surprise, almost hitting his hairline. "What?.." and then he starts to laugh.

"Ally, I'm not gay. I just won't do this when you're inebriated," He is says, saying all the right things, but I'm drowning in tequila and hurt.

"Fuck you, Jackson! I'll just take care of myself!" I snap, storming off and locking myself in the bathroom again. I collapse onto the floor, curled into a ball. The weight of the last twenty-four hours crashes down on me, and I can't hold back the tears. They come pouring out, salty and heavy streaming down my face.

"What the actual fuck just happened?" He doesn't sound angry—more worried. But I feel like a complete idiot.

"Just go away," I manage between sobs.

"Why are you crying?"

I can't bring myself to answer. I'm too embarrassed.

Broken

"Ally, talk to me. I'm not going anywhere until you do," he insists. His concern hangs thick in the air. Time drags. When he finally speaks again, frustration's creeps into his tone.

"Why would you tell your sister I'm gay?" he shouts, and my heart sinks.

—Tyler's here? That can't be right.

"Yeah, well, she's locked herself in the fucking bathroom crying and won't come out," he continues. He must be on the phone. After the way things went down earlier, it was only a matter of time before Tyler reached out, and Jax must have picked up my phone.

"Well, go on then," he says. There's something undeniably attractive about his anger—but I quickly push that thought away. He already turned me down once tonight.

"Banana, what's going on?" Ty's voice cuts through from the other side of the door.

"Don't call me that!" I snap.

"Jax, check the calendar on the fridge. What date has the asterisks?" he pushes and I can feel my temper flaring.

Broken

"Fuck you, Tyler. I do not have PMS!" I yell at the door like it personally insulted me.

"So help me god! You've got five seconds to tell me what he did before I drive down there and kick the shit out of his face!"

He's got some nerve to threaten Jax when he's the reason I'm a wreck. I stay silent, refusing to give him the satisfaction of a response.

"HANNAH!" he roars.

"He won't have sex with me!"

After that outburst, I swear I'm done drinking for good. Someone mutters "Jesus" under their breath—I don't know which of them.

"It's all your fault!" I'm spiralling, and I know it but I'm too far gone to care.

"I didn't do anything, you're just too drunk—"

"NOT YOU. HIM!"

"Ally, you know I didn't mean—"

"Fuck you, Ty! This is all your fault! Life is your fault—and tequila too! I'm blaming you for tequila!"

Broken

"What the fuck did you say to her?" Jax snaps, rage flaring again. I can feel the burn of his glare through the door.

"Seriously, what the actual fuck is wrong with your family? I respect her too much to pressure her, therefore I must be gay and now she feels rejected? Fuck this!" he yells, and I hear his footsteps stomp away and realise I've finally pushed him away.

I hear drawers being yanked open. Is he seriously rummaging through my kitchen right now? Poor guy must really needs a drink after the chat we just had.

Then I hear the bathroom handle jiggle. The lock clicks open.

Suddenly, I'm lifted off the floor and draped across Jax's lap as he sits on the tiles. My head rests on his shoulder, my hand on his chest, right above his heart. The steady beat calms the storm inside me. He strokes my hair a few times before breaking the silence.

"Tell me what he said," he murmurs softly into my hair.

"If you were dating someone normal, he'd think you were gay after your balls turned blue," I mumble.

Broken

"Jesus! You know I'm going to hit him, right?"

"You can't hit him for being right," I reply.

He gently tilts my chin up, making me meet his eyes.

"He's not right. Take it from someone who used to think with their cock. If he cared about someone, he wouldn't think that way."

When I don't respond, he brushes my tear-streaked cheeks with his thumb.

"We'll get there when you're ready—and it won't be because of tequila or your fucking brother," he says firmly.

The air between us is thick with intensity, honesty, and compassion. Our breath is the only sound as I look into this incredible man's eyes and realise—I'm falling in love with him.

CHAPTER 19

I wake up the next morning nestled against Jax, my head resting on his chest while he gently plays with my hair. I snuggle in a bit closer, and he leans down to plant a soft kiss on the top of my head.

"How are you feeling?" he asks.

"Like I downed half a bottle of tequila," I groan.

"You did." He chuckles, trying—and failing—not to laugh outright.

Broken

The events of last night are a bit of a blur; I can't recall much after that fourth shot.

"How much do I need to apologise for?" I ask, half-joking.

"To me? Nothing. But you might have traumatised your brother for life," he teases.

"Why? I remember parts of it, but a lot of it's fuzzy." My heart races at the thought of what I might have said.

"Well, you kind of blamed him for me not taking advantage of you right before you yelled at him about not having PMS, then told him that life and tequila were all his fault."

I bury my face in Jax's chest, mortified, while he laughs. After a moment of silence, I realise there's something more pressing I need to bring up.

"You never asked why he calls me Hannah," I say, sensing the question looming.

His fingers still in my hair, and his body stiffens slightly. "I figured you'd tell me if you wanted me to know."

Broken

"It's my name. Its why everyone calls me Banana, Ty couldn't say Hannah when we were little so it became Banana."

His fingers start stroking my hair again, but he stays quiet.

"Alison's my middle name; I started going by Ally when I moved here."

"Why?" he asks.

"Because I didn't want to be Hannah anymore."

"Okay… is there anything else important I should know about you?"

I think about revealing that I spent months not leaving my house, that the inside of my head is far more fucked up than I let him see, and that I'm falling in love with him, but I decide to keep those thoughts to myself..

"No. Anything I should know about you?" I counter.

"Nothing too important," he replies.

He kisses the top of my head again, and we stay wrapped up together on my bed for another hour, savouring the moment, until Jax has to head back home for work.

Broken

The first thing I do when he leaves is schedule an emergency Zoom session with Jeanie.

◆ ◆ ◆

It's Thursday morning, and I'm finally starting to feel like my old self again. After a few days of uneventful calm, I'm genuinely thankful for the boredom—especially after the chaotic weekend I just endured. I know the police will try to contact me again soon regarding the incident, but I'm putting off thinking about that for as long as possible. This morning, I even ventured out of my apartment to grab coffee, so I'm focusing on my progress.

Jax has been busy with a work project, so I haven't seen him since he left on Tuesday morning, but he checks in on me every few hours in a way that feels supportive rather than intrusive. He sends me random questions throughout the day, which keeps the conversation flowing without directly asking how I'm holding up emotionally.

Broken

On Wednesday, I finally got around to returning Tyler's calls, but I stood my ground and didn't apologise—even for blaming him for everything. I knew I probably should have, but it just didn't feel right, so I decided to let it go and act like it never happened. Surprisingly, he was cool with that and mentioned that Jax had been keeping him updated on my wellbeing—which I didn't even know he had the contact info for. I have to admit, I'm comforted by their interactions. They might even end up being friends one day.

Later that evening, I felt the need for a distraction, so I hopped online to bid on some projects. There were the usual themes like fey and vampires, plus a particularly bizarre listing about bestiality from a cow's perspective that I quickly scrolled past. A few projects caught my eye, so I placed some bids and decided to call it a night. After a refreshing shower, I settled into bed, ready to unwind, when my phone buzzed with a text. I figured it was just Jax saying goodnight, so I didn't think much of it as I slipped into my pyjamas.

But then I read his message.

Broken

Jax: I miss the way your pussy tastes.

Christ on a cracker!

That was unexpected! I've never received anything like that before. While dirty talk isn't really my thing, I can't help but feel a rush from his words. I wanted to respond without having to contribute much, but still encourage him to continue.

So, I shoot back, *How do I taste*? The moment I hit send, I regret it.

Do I really want to know the answer to that?

Jax: Hot and sweet like sugar. You're my favourite flavour.

Ally: Even more than peanut butter?

Jax: Peanut butter doesn't even compare to the taste of you when you melt on my tongue.

Honestly, I'm at a loss. My new vibrator finally showed up yesterday, but I haven't had the guts to take it out of the box yet. I get out of bed and go to my cupboard, where it's stashed away like a little secret I'm embarrassed about. When I finally open it, I realise it's not as intimidating as I'd imagined. I snap a quick photo and send it to Jax as a response, but then my

Broken

phone rings almost instantly. I freak out and hit reject before I even think it through.

Jax: Feeling a bit shy? Haha, that's ok, you don't have to talk. Just put the phone next to your head on speaker so I can hear you while you touch yourself.

I mull it over and figure it's not such a bad idea; I'll be so aware of him being there that I'll probably stay quiet, and he'll just catch the sounds of the vibrations. I call him back, and he picks up on the first ring.

"Hey, beautiful. Have you not done this before?"

"No."

"That's alright, we'll take it slow. Just lie back and set the phone on speaker next to your head."

His voice sends shivers down my spine. I'm already breathless, and I haven't even turned the thing on yet.

God, how does he make me feel this undone with just his voice?

"Are you comfortable?"

"Yes," I'm barely able to get the word out, my voice just a soft murmur.

Broken

"Hold off on turning it on for now. Start with just your fingers. Use one hand to pinch your nipple and let the other slide into your panties."

"I'm not wearing any," I say, thinking it's just a logistical detail, but the way he groans on the other end tells me I might have struck a much sexier chord than I meant to.

"Are you already wet, beautiful?" he asks, and I slide two fingers down to check, always wanting to be thorough, and respond truthfully.

"Yes."

"Rub your clit—slow and gentle. Pretend it's my fingers."

A soft sound escapes me, unsure if it's from the sensation or his voice.

I shouldn't be this turned on by just his words… but here I am, melting like butter.

"God, Ally. I'm so hard for you. My cock is throbbing in my hand," he admits, and the thought of him pleasuring himself sends a wave of heat through me, making me moan.

Broken

"You loved it when I teased your clit, my tongue dancing over it while I pulled that orgasm right out of you," he continues, and I can't help but think he's trying to drive me wild with his words.

"Now let go of that nipple you better still be playing with and grab the vibrator."

I hit the power button, and it hums to life in my palm.

God, I hope I'm doing this right.

"Good girl. Now place the tip of it on your clit."

I'm overwhelmed with sensation the moment it hits me, and I can feel my breath quickening.

Oh wow—okay—that's intense.

"Stay still; just keep it there until I tell you to move," he instructs.

The way his voice resonates with the vibrations is pushing me closer to the edge faster than I can handle.

"Alright, stop now; you're warmed up."

Warmed up? Who's he kidding? I was on the brink of release! I let out a frustrated groan, which only makes him chuckle. Jerk.

Broken

"Good girl. Now, run your fingers through your folds, get them nice and slick, and slowly slide two inside."

Turns out I have a praise kink I didn't know about, because hearing 'good girl' sends shivers down my spine.

"How do you feel? Are you wet for me, beautiful?"

"So wet," I manage to whisper, lost in a moan. I've never felt this wanted. This known.

"When you're ready, turn the vibrator on, but don't put it in; I want to be the one to stretch you. Just hold it against your clit. Don't take too long; I'm ready to come, but I'm waiting for you."

I've been so caught up in my own pleasure that I didn't realise his breathing had quickened and his voice is strained. I hit the power button again, and the device springs back to life, making me cry out.

Oh god, I'm already so close.

"That's it, beautiful, get nice and wet with your fingers for me. Push deeper, just like I do.

Broken

"Jesus, Ally, I'm so close. I can't help but picture your lips around my cock. You look incredible with my cock in your mouth.

"Come with me, beautiful; be a good girl and let go for me."

I moan his name as my legs start to shake, and I find myself holding my breath. I clench around my fingers, coming harder than I ever thought possible without his touch.

Fuck, that was intense. He really knows how to unravel me.

"Jesus, Ally. You make the sexiest sounds when you come.

Are you still there?"

"Hmm."

His laughter resonates with a rich, warm tone that's just bursting with joy.

"Get some sleep, beautiful. I'll call you tomorrow."

"Good night," I reply, feeling a bit shy for some reason, my voice struggling to work.

"Oh, and Ally?"

"Yeah?"

Broken

"I'll be dreaming about you."

Honestly, this guy sends my heart racing. There's something so sweet and caring about him that just makes everything feel special. And damn it, he even knows my taste—better than peanut butter.

Broken

CHAPTER 20

It's Friday arvo, and Jax hasn't reached out at all—not even his usual midday questions. It's strange. He's only ever skipped one day since we had that chat about condiments, just a couple of days after we first met. By 2 PM, I shoot him a message to check in, but there's still no response, which is really unlike him. As the clock edges closer to 4, a knot of worry tightens in my stomach, so I give him a call. When he picks up, his tone is... off.

"Yes, Ally?" he says, and I'm immediately thrown.

"Umm, hi?" I reply, unsure.

"Is that a question?" he snaps, and I'm taken aback.

"What? No. Hi—how are you?" I try to keep it light, but he bites back.

"Better at minding my own business than you, apparently."

Whoa. What the fuck?

"Is something wrong?" I ask, genuinely concerned.

"Why would I advertise my problems to you?" he shoots back, and I'm left stunned. This isn't the Jax I know. He's been blunt, sure, but never rude. I'm scrambling to figure out what I could've done when he sighs heavily.

"I'm sorry. I'm dealing with a work crisis. I'm not fit to talk to you right now. Let me call you tomorrow."

"O-okay," I manage, confusion and concern colliding inside me.

"I miss you, beautiful," he adds, and despite myself, I smile a little.

"I miss you too," I say, but after we hang up, I'm more puzzled than ever. This side of him is completely foreign to me, and guilt creeps in. I can't blame him for having a rough day—he's seen me through enough of my own meltdowns.

I send a goodnight text as I crawl into bed, but there's no reply. It leaves me uneasy. It's hard to fall asleep with this whirlpool of worry swirling around in my head.

When I wake the next morning, there's a weird feeling in my gut I can't quite shake. Like I'm waiting for something to drop. The lack of his usual morning message only ramps up my anxiety, and no matter how much I try to distract myself, my mind races with worst-case scenarios.

By midday, when my phone finally buzzes, I nearly drop it.

Jax: If you could have any superpower, what
would it be?

Ally: Elemental control. You?

Jax: Empathy.

Ally: Empathy's not a superpower. And you're
not lacking in it, not even a little.

What a weird answer. He can't be serious. He's the most empathetic man I've ever known.

Broken

Jax: Just heading into an important lunch
meeting. Dinner with me?

Ally: Can't tonight. I've got two drafts due
Monday—gonna take me all weekend.

Jax: Monday night then?

Ally: Love to.

Jax: I'll pick you up at 7 after the gym. I'd skip
it, but I'll need to burn off some steam
before I see you.

Ally: Wait—you're in a suit right now, aren't
you?

Jax: Haha, no. Not today. But if you're planning
to objectify me, I'll throw one on Monday.

Ally: I don't need a reason for that. I do it all the
time.

When he doesn't reply straight away, I dive back into my latest project—something about a housewife by day, killer pigeon trainer by night. Still need to tackle the other one, about a farmer who suffers from anatidaephobia—the irrational fear that a duck, somewhere, is watching you.

Seriously, who comes up with this stuff?

Broken

It's nearly dark by the time I wrap things up on Monday. Oddly enough, *The Eye of the Duck* turned out to be a cracking good script, though it took me forever to finish—my thoughts kept wandering back to Jax. Somehow, in such a short time, he's turned my world on its head. He makes me feel like I'm floating. Safe. Seen. Loved. It's almost surreal. I never thought someone like him could exist outside of fiction. He's thoughtful, kind, patient—everything a girl could want. And somehow, he wants me, flaws and all. For years I believed the closest I'd get to a real relationship would be with the fictional men in my books. But Jax? He makes them look like amateurs.

I glance at the clock—he'll be here in forty minutes. I leap off the couch and dart to the shower.

Just as I'm drying my hair, still wrapped in a towel, the intercom buzzes. *Shit.* He's early. I scramble to finish up, and when the knock sounds at the door, I'm still not dressed. I fling it open and he takes me in with that slow, wicked grin, his eyes trailing up from my toes making me bite my lip in response.

Broken

He steps inside, shuts the door behind him, and cups my face, kissing me like I'm the air he needs to breathe. His tongue teases mine, his lips so skilled I'm left breathless, clinging to his shirt as our foreheads press together.

"God, I missed you," he sighs.

"I missed you too."

"I'm really sorry for being such a rude dick the other day. I feel terrible."

"Don't be silly. I caught you at a bad time. It must've been annoying."

"Ally, you could never annoy me." He exhales, eyes locking with mine. "I love you, Ally. You don't have to say it back, but I need you to know—I'm falling in love with you."

I stare at him, completely undone.

"I love you too."

I've been aware my feelings for Jax must be almost like love, and honestly, it's a whole new experience for me. The depth of my emotions for him is hard to put into words; it's just so intense and unlike anything I've ever felt before, but I never anticipated that he would feel such a strong connection to me as well. There's an overwhelming sense of safety that envelops me when I'm with him, and the realisation that he might love me is almost too much for my mind to handle.

"I want you."

"Ally, no. That's not why I said it."

I cant help but smile, "I know. I'd want you even if you hadn't said it," I say, drawing closer, inhaling his familiar sandalwood scent.

"Are you sure? We don't have to rush. I'll wait until you're ready."

"Shut up and kiss me," I insist, tugging him closer by his shirt. Our lips crash together in a kiss that's hot, urgent, and aching with something deeper. He responds instantly, kissing me back like he's starved for it, hands sliding into my hair, gripping gently like he's afraid I might vanish.

He pulls away, breath shaky, eyes blazing yet soft. They flicker between mine like he's searching for something unspoken.

Broken

"We're going to take this slow, in case you change your mind," he says, voice low, steady. "Because once I have you, you're mine. I'm never letting you go."

He leans in closer, kissing me with a softness that feels both tender and deliberate. His lips trail along my jawline and down my neck, sending shivers through me. His hands find their way to my hips, pulling me closer until I can feel his arousal pressing against my stomach. Our lips reconnect in a gentle, yet passionate, kiss. As I step back, he follows, keeping our mouths locked until we reach my bedroom, stopping at the foot of the bed. I quickly rip his shirt over his head and unbutton his jeans, pushing them down and watching as he steps out of them and reaches for the towel wrapped around me. He looks at me for a moment, seeking my approval, before pulling it away. With both hands on my back, he guides me to lie down on the bed, and we shuffle until we're in the centre—him hovering above me, supporting himself on his hands.

"You can still change your mind," he whispers.

Broken

I think about it for a fleeting second but there's no doubt in my head, no fear. Only trust so I shake my head.

"Use your words, Ally."

"I want you."

He leans over to grab a condom from his wallet, sets it aside, and returns to me. As he kisses me gently, his hands start to wander, smoothly tracing over my chest before pausing to tease my nipple, then moving down to my hips and eventually resting between my thighs.

"You're so wet for me, beautiful," he whispers, sliding a finger inside me, and I can't help but moan into his mouth. He picks up the pace, adding another finger while his mouth finds my nipple, teasing it with his tongue before sucking it gently. My back arches as pleasure radiates from my nipple straight to where his fingers are working their magic, his thumb rubbing against my clit. I feel the tension build within me, and as I come, I breathe his name. He removes his fingers, bringing them to his mouth to savour me, then tenderly strokes my cheek. Tucking my hair behind my ear, he kisses me softly—and my heart races with anticipation when he asks, "You ready?"

"Yes."

He positions himself between my legs, tearing open the condom with his teeth before rolling it down his impressive length. I can't help but watch, transfixed, as his hand glides the latex over himself. With that playful smirk I adore, he leans in closer and says, "I'll go slow." His movements are practiced, but there's nothing rushed about him. He positions himself at my entrance, eyes locked on mine.

"I'm going to be gentle with you, but it still might hurt. Tell me the moment it's too much, or if you want me to stop."

He lines himself up, then adds, "Keep your eyes on me." Slowly, he begins to push inside.

He presses in with painstaking care, moving inch by inch, pulling back before easing in deeper. His eyes stay fixed on mine as he lowers his forehead to rest against me. The initial pressure is manageable, but as he delves deeper, it sharpens into pain. I inhale sharply, trying to resist the urge to pull away.

Broken

"You're doing so well, beautiful. Just breathe. Try to relax," he soothes.

"Are you in?" I ask, my voice strained with discomfort.

"Halfway. God, you feel so fucking good… incredible," he groans, jaw clenched. "You're so tight around me. I won't last long," he admits.

He pauses, giving me a moment to adjust before pulling back and pressing in again. My eyes squeeze shut, and I grip his biceps tightly.

He holds still, letting me settle. When he moves again, it's only a little—back, then deeper. I focus on breathing through the sensation, clinging to his arms.

"Almost there. Stay with me, Ally. Keep your eyes open," he urges.

His voice anchors me. I glance up, catching his handsome, strained expression, and realise just how much control he's using to keep this slow.

"You can move," I say, surprised by the sound of my own voice.

"Not yet. I don't want to hurt you." He kisses me softly, murmuring against my lips, and the way he's watching me—with patience, with reverence—makes everything feel safe.

But as I begin to relax and sink into the mattress, the pain fades into something more bearable. I shift my hips, and he sucks in a sharp breath before kissing me again—slow and careful. I move beneath him, and he groans, eyes fluttering shut.

"God, you feel like heaven. I'm going to move slowly. Just tell me if it's too much," he murmurs.

He pulls back slightly, then pushes in again. The ache begins to melt into warmth.

He finds a gentle rhythm, each stroke easing the sting until it dissolves into heat. I feel so connected to him, so full of him. As he picks up the pace, I start to move with him—just as his thumb finds my clit, drawing tight, deliberate circles.

"Oh God… don't stop."

The intensity builds with every movement. My core throbs, my stomach tightens, and my breath comes in sharp bursts.

"That's it, beautiful. Be a good girl and let go for me."

Broken

His words, his scent, the weight of him—it's all too much. My thighs wrap tightly around his hips, and I cling to his arms, lost in the moment as he guides me through wave after wave until I'm nothing but a satisfied puddle beneath him.

He keeps moving, his pace quickening. Then he pinches my clit, and I gasp.

"Don't stop," I breathe. It's building fast, making me clench around him, again.

"That's it Ally, soak my cock again."

His voice, his body, his scent—they overwhelm me. I come again, legs locking around him, pulling him closer.

Not long after, he follows—tensing with a sharp curse before collapsing on top of me, completely spent. He tilts his head, pressing a soft kiss to my cheek, then pulls back slightly to check on me.

"You okay?"

I nod, smiling. "Better than okay."

He grins, presses another kiss to my lips.

"You're so perfect," I tell him, feeling like my heart is ready to explode.

Broken

He chuckles and replies, "Aren't all firemen?" which makes me burst into laughter.

He slowly pulls out of me, and I feel a pang of emptiness, instantly missing that connection. He heads to the bathroom to dispose of the condom, leaving me to sit up and survey my body. Everything looks the same, yet it feels so different. I feel lighter, as if a huge weight has been lifted. Like something broken inside me has finally started to heal.

There's no trace of panic, anxiety, or fear—just a deep sense of relief and satisfaction.

He returns and sits down on the bed beside me, completely at ease naked, while I instinctively cross my arms over my chest. It's funny how, after everything we've just shared, I suddenly feel shy around him. He chuckles softly, shaking his head at my insecurity, but he doesn't say anything about it.

"What's that look?" he asks, brushing his thumb along my cheek.

"I was just thinking… I wish you'd been my first."

Broken

Something flickers in his eyes. Sadness? Regret? But then he smiles and tucks a strand of hair behind my ear.

"Are you sore?"

"A little." I reply being honest.

"Do you still want to go for dinner?"

"I'm never leaving this bed."

He chuckles and then leans over to grab his phone from his pants on the floor and places an order for delivery. We eat half-dressed, tangled in sheets and each other. He makes love to me again, slow and sweet. I fall asleep with my head on his chest, lulled by his heartbeat.

◆ ◆ ◆

I wake up in the morning feeling elated. My body is pleasantly sore, a reminder of the night before, and my heart feels both full and light, as if I could just lift off the ground at any moment. The thought of him loving me fills me with joy. It takes a second for me to realise that I'm in bed alone, but I brush it off without a second thought. I stretch out my arms and legs, then curl back up, waiting for Jax to finish up in the bathroom or deal with whatever work crisis popped up this time. I'm sure he knows he can use my laptop if he needs to, so I don't feel the need to disturb him. After a few minutes, I start to notice the silence in the apartment, which feels a bit unsettling. I gingerly get out of bed, half-expecting to float away on the wave of happiness coursing through me, and reach for his T-shirt, only to find it missing.

Oddly enough, his jeans and shoes are nowhere to be found either.

Maybe he stepped out to grab some coffee from down the street?

I snatch my phone from the bedside table and try to call him, hoping he can pick me up something to eat too—apparently, after a night like that, hunger hits hard. The call doesn't even ring before I'm met with his voicemail. His phone probably died from not being charged last night. I pull on pyjamas to avoid being caught in the nude when he returns and walk out to the living room.

Broken

As I enter the room, I notice that the dried rose in the Gembrook Hill bottle has been moved from the window seal to the edge of the counter, and in front of it lies a folded piece of paper standing upright that simply reads,

It was a pleasure fucking you, Ally. ~J x.

Suddenly, the air feels heavy, and a chill runs through me; my mouth goes dry. My heart starts racing in a way that feels completely off.

No.

He wouldn't just leave, would he? I scan the page again, and then once more, trying to wrap my head around what's happening, but it's like trying to catch smoke with my bare hands. He's gone? I already know the answer before I dash back to my room, grabbing my phone to call him yet again.

It's off—*he's gone*.

Those two words play over and over again in my head as I slide down the wall and curl up on the floor, still holding onto the phone like it's a lifeline. No tears fall just yet; I can feel them lurking, but for now, it's just a heavy silence filled with my thoughts.

Broken

Why?

How?

Did I miss something?

What the actual fuck is happening right now?

Is this some kind of joke and I'm missing the punch line?

Am I the punchline here?

What could possibly make him do this?

Why go through all that trouble only to disappear?

Why tell me he *loves* me?

Why would he make me fall in love with him?

The questions race through my mind, each one slamming into me like a freight train. I shut my eyes as the first tears begin to fall, and I find myself stuck drowning in hopelessness, trying to make sense of what's happening.

Just like that. He wasn't coming back.

And I was breaking.

Again.

THE END

Broken

Also by Margaux Paris

Broken - Damaged Hearts 1

Flawed - Damaged Hearts 2

Wounded - A Damaged Hearts Story

Broken

227

Broken

About The Author

Margaux Paris is a Sydney-based author of dark romance and emotionally charged contemporary fiction. A lifelong romance reader with a love for morally grey men, broken heroines, and stories that walk the tightrope between ruin and redemption, Margaux never imagined she'd one day be on the other side of the page. It wasn't until her husband gently nudged her to take a chance that she finally put pen to paper—and discovered that writing the book she could never quite find on the shelf was exactly where she was meant to be.

What started as a deeply personal passion project slowly evolved into the Damaged Hearts Duet, a raw, unflinching story about love, loss, obsession, and the complicated path toward healing. With Broken and Flawed, Margaux invites readers into a world of emotional chaos, layered characters, and love that doesn't always play fair—but always leaves a mark.

When she's not writing or sneaking in late-night reading sessions, Margaux is a proud mum to three wild and wonderful young boys who keep her on her

Broken

toes (and her coffee intake dangerously high). Fuelled by caffeine, V Energy Drink, and an ever-growing obsession with fictional men—Joey Lynch being the gold standard—she finds inspiration in the beautifully flawed characters that live in her head long before they make it to the page.

Margaux is currently working on Wounded, a spin-off in the Damaged Hearts universe that dives into the story of an emotionally repressed mechanic and the girl he never really let go.

Broken

Afterword

Thank you for making it to the end of Broken. This was the first book I ever wrote. The beginning of everything. I had no idea where it would take me— only that I needed to write it. That I needed to tell this story.

Jax and Ally's world came alive long before I had the courage to share it. Their pain, their pull, their chaos—it became the heartbeat of my debut. Raw, messy, imperfect. Just like them.

This book was never meant to be easy. It was meant to be honest. For the ones who have been broken and still find the strength to care. To trust. To love. Even when it hurts.

If any part of this story stayed with you, cracked something open or made you feel seen—thank you. You gave this debut its meaning.

And if you're still standing at the end of it, just know:

Broken was only the beginning.

—Margaux Paris

Broken

Acknowledgments

Writing a book is a deeply personal process, but bringing one into the world takes a village—and I'm lucky to have had some of the best.

To my husband—thank you for enduring months of me talking about Jax as if he were real (because let's face it, he kind of is). For listening to my endless rants about morally grey men, complicated plot twists, and emotionally loaded scenes—thank you for always being in my corner, no matter how obsessed I got.

To my favourite book friend—you know who you are. Thank you for loving swoon-worthy fictional boyfriends as fiercely as I do and for being there through the chaos of the last few months. Your support, sarcasm, and late-night messages meant more than you know.

To my editor, CJ Editing—thank you for your patience and your urgency, in equal measure. For your hilarious feedback, for catching what I missed, and for treating this story with care and clarity. I'm so grateful.

To my incredible ARC readers—thank you for falling

Broken

for Jax the way I did. Your early support, excitement, and kind words gave this book its heartbeat. Knowing he lived in your minds the way he lived in mine means everything.

And to you, dear reader—thank you for taking a chance on a story about love, trauma, obsession, and healing. I hope it stays with you long after the final page.

Broken